"Love, hope, joy, peace, family, friends, tradition: We all look for these calming influences on our lives. Fortunately, we don't have to look very far when we have a quiet cup of coffee and a Kirsten Chapman column in our hands. Kirsten has a way with words that allows us to celebrate year round."

-- TOMMIE RAMSEY, Columbus, Ohio, 1995

"Kirsten Chapman writes beautifully."

-- JAMES J. KILPATRICK, syndicated columnist, 1993

"I look forward to her observations and musing on everyday things. It's like a breath of fresh air, a pause in our busy lives to read about feelings about family, etc., which we all experience or think about but never put down on paper."

-- MYRA SARKADI, Worthington, Ohio, 1997

"There is about the work of Kirsten Chapman an eloquent but quiet grace. She is a fine and gifted writer. . . . Go back to her blackberry summers, feel the heft of the black physician's bag her father carried about the Wisconsin countryside to tend the cradle-to-grave aches and fevers of his medical pastorate. Her life is the perfume of peonies, the tides within us governed by moonrise and moonset, the feel of gathering dusk on Christmas Eve when all that matters is that the runners of the sled are cutting a lazy arc through the mantle of snow toward home."

-- MIKE HARDEN, columnist, *The Columbus Dispatch*, 1998

Leif Lokvam
Summer, 1947

The Way Home

Kirsten Chapman

Illustrations by Patti Sharpe

Foreword by Mike Harden

THIRD TREE PRESS

Published by Third Tree Press, Ft. Lauderdale, Florida
Library of Congress Card Catalogue Number: 98-061049
ISBN 0-9665767-0-5
www.chapmanthewayhome.com

THIRD TREE PRESS

TO THE WHEEL OF FAMILY
AND A JOURNEY CALLED LOVE.

To my husband, Erie,
and children, Tyler and Tia.
To my parents, Leif and Marian Lokvam,
and sisters and brother, Karen, Sonja and Chris.

Acknowledgments

With special thanks to *The Columbus Dispatch.*

And to Luke Feck, Bob Smith and Mike Curtin for publishing my work.

To T.R. Fitchko for believing in the essays before I did and including them in Accent.

To Margie Breckenridge and Tracy Lemmon for their patient teaching.

To Mike Harden for his foreword, encouragement and the pleasure of his columns.

To Evangelia Philippidis for her assistance.

To Gary Kiefer for accepting my first free-lance articles in *Capitol* magazine.

And to Kirk Arnott, Joe Blundo, Kitty Harriel, Jewell Johnson, Becky Kover, Jim Massie, Scott Minister, John McNeely, Lisa Reuter, Mark Siple and many others for their help over the years.

Special thanks to friends who assisted and encouraged: Carole Banta, Jan Garlock, Susan Quintenz, Babs Sirak, Sue VanDyke and Julie Wilkins.

To Dar Hayes, who coordinated the project.
To Anita Mitchell, who typed -- and typed.
To Bob and Tim Andersen, who produced this book.

To Patti Sharpe, who painted my words and captured what I couldn't.

And to Jean Goldsmith, who always said "the book will happen." And, because of her, it did.

There are all those early memories;
one cannot get another set.

WILLA CATHER

Essays

Foreword

To write is to taste life twice, someone once said: first in the moment we live it, again in the narrative tapestry memory weaves of prose. The first taste is the sweetest, but it is the second over which we linger.

When we are children, life is a Monet we view with our noses three inches from the canvas. Each experience is a pastel explosion, a brushstroke that -- though it scintillates with the joy or sorrow of the moment -- is totally without context. To live, then, is to take the baby steps backward, watching as distance melds form and shape, and the splotches become a flower garden.

Something in the essays of Kirsten Chapman reminds me of E.B. White's favorite lake in Maine. He had been taken there as a boy by his father in 1904. He loved that lake as only a child can love; yet, when he returned to it with his own son, Joel, it was a different lake he saw. The chill that had been a mere lift in the wind on the water in his youth had become figurative when he felt it as a father inching toward middle age. It was an intimation of his mortality. Such psychic nudges stir us in diverse ways. Some panic or mourn lost youth. Some take lovers half their age. The writer -- aware that God is in the details -- inspects the jumble of disparate pieces and begins to fit them together. If the crafting of personal essays appears --

to the casual observer -- a self-indulgently solitary act, the publishing of them is, at once, both generous and frightening. In making the personal universal, we are a little like prospectors, knocking shards of mineral from the walls of shadowy caves and hoping the assayers (our readers) will find worth in our labors.

There is about the work of Kirsten Chapman an eloquent but quiet grace. She is a fine and gifted writer. That alone, however, is insufficient to distill from life its essence and entice the reader to partake. That requires heart and self-lessness, cliched though that may sound. The proof, of course, is in the reading of Chapman's work. Go back to her blackberry summers, feel the heft of the black physician's bag her father carried about the Wisconsin countryside to tend the cradle-to-grave aches and fevers of his medical pastorate. Her life is the perfume of peonies, the tides within us governed by moonrise and moonset, the feel of gathering dusk on Christmas Eve when all that matters is that the runners of the sled are cutting a lazy arc through the mantle of snow toward home.

To read Chapman is to understand what the monks mean when they talk about the Buddhist ideal of living a totally conscious life. It is our great fortune that she has taken the time to write it down.

Mike Harden
July, 1998

The Back Door

Don't ignore the back door. It grows in significance long after a front door's summer geraniums or winter wreath fades from memory. Spruce up the scene. Apply a fresh coat of paint. Take care how you act and react there. It may be a far more important place than you ever dreamed.

My mother first pointed this out: "Have you ever noticed," she asked, "how it's the people you care for the most who use the back door?

"The front door seems destined for salespeople, strangers and acquaintances," she said, "not for family or closest friends."

If some of life's more poignant exits and entrances occur at the rear of the house, perhaps that's because it's often closer to the car, the bike -- the natural passageway to our daily path.

Whatever the reason, all I need is one slight push at memory's portal and the images revolve: I hear the slap of a screen door as I escape the neighbor boys' water pistols; the snip, snip of shears as my father prunes the nearby privet hedge. At the eternal back door he magically reappeared each evening; my mother rescued me from sitters; my baby brother made his first entry into our home. It offered freedom on summer mornings, refuge on snowy nights and solace when the big kids wouldn't let me play.

At age seven, I moved to another house. Next to the back door was a milk chute with a little door. Though milk was no longer delivered, my older sister Sonja and I found multiple uses for the small compartment -- a place to stash our workbooks or roller skates or even notes to each other.

Years later, all three of us sisters, dressed in white, left for our weddings through the back door. After my children were born, I carried them through this same passageway to meet their grandparents.

On January 12, 1977, the day we buried my thirty-six-year-old sister, Sonja, the temperature was minus twelve degrees, so cold that for the first time we had to cover the kitchen window with a Hudson Bay blanket. As we left through our back door for the funeral, I glimpsed the milk chute and wished I could leave one more note.

Different back doors, different memories: I see my first-born mounting his red two-wheeler for the first day of first grade, my daughter's crayon drawing -- like that of an ancient cave-dweller's -- left for posterity on the adjoining garage wall.

Both children ventured forth from back doors -- to school, to camp, to college -- and returned again and again, daughter into woman, son into man. Locking the door each night throughout their vast, but brief, childhoods, I studied the constant stars and changing moon.

Some doors stand open -- waiting to close. I remember my teen-age self sitting at my aunt's kitchen table.

"He and I'd been having breakfast right here," she

recalled. "We talked about the babies, his flight plan for the day. Then he rose, gave me a kiss and went out the back door. 'Love you,' he said through the screen and gave a wave. Then he was gone."

The phone rang a few hours later, she said: "A crash . . . no survivors . . . burned beyond recognition."

My middle-aged aunt fiddled with the corner of her napkin, remembering: "Since I never saw him afterwards, my last memory is a happy one -- when he turned and waved goodbye. Sometimes," she said, smiling, "I still think he's going to open that back door and walk back in."

An uncle I never knew, parents I love, children and siblings no longer young -- held as they once were behind a scrim. All are there on the threshold, gathered once more, whenever I tug at memory's back door.

The Way Home

The way home is along a road, the open road of high-way.

"Why don't you fly?" ask friends, incredulous that I still prefer to drive in an era of discount fares.

I want to return to Wisconsin at my own speed, in my own time; to leave one back door and -- eight hours later -- arrive at another. I need to pass through the countryside, not fly over it; to drive myself instead of being delivered.

With summer fields like a quilt spread out before me, I can't resist traveling an open road or seeing the farms that call like far-off fiddle music.

"Take along some talking books," a friend suggested, "to make it less boring." How could she possibly know that the tapes inside my head are the ones I want to hear again -- stories about my mother's farm and my own memories of Hannans' farm, where we boarded my sister's horse.

Outside Columbus, Ohio, I feel city and stress slip away as I spot not only red-winged blackbirds but also a red

Chevy truck with two white-necked ducks and two black-necked ducks craning to look out the back window. Everywhere, pockets of pink flowers and blue ones border the highway. If I were flying, I'd miss it all.

Downtown workers in Columbus would be heading to lunch right now, jamming Broad and High. In Indiana, a riderless blue tractor rests in a field. For miles, one red barn after another looms ahead; in the distance, over a corn sea, three white barns bob on the horizon.

When my mother was growing up on a farm in Wisconsin, she'd help carry water and food to those working in the field. As she grew older, she labored alongside her father, sister and brothers, planting and stripping tobacco, fretting over what price it would bring at auction.

Yet, all was not bleak. In a barn like the ones I now rush by, she found sweet watermelon in the cold-water tank, and large jars of her mother's homemade root beer -- the best, she says, she has tasted.

Thirteen miles outside of Indianapolis, I see clouds gather. The air holds its breath; suddenly, troughs of rain spill down. A horse trailer with hay on top finds refuge under an overpass. Still, like the sixteen-wheeler from Fargo, North Dakota, in front of me, I press on.

At this moment, no one in the world knows exactly where I am -- just as they didn't when I'd find shelter in the Hannans' hayloft before a summer storm. Climbing to celestial, choir-loft heights, I'd leave the barn's nave and aisle below. Light filtering through dusty windows and worn timbers cast a stained-glass glow.

Hiding in that hush, between morning and afternoon chores, I could hear -- from someplace higher -- a soft beating of wings. Then, suddenly, from even higher, came rumbling and crackling thunder.

Other times, I'd play ship as the barn heaved and

5

creaked, rain slashing its dark windows. Like Noah's, my ark was stashed with provisions -- piles of hay and bales of straw, oats as warm as sand; an animal inside each stall; and best of all were the stowaway kittens in the hayloft.

Eventually the sun returned, lighting everything.

So, too, during my long car ride, the rain ceases. Over a Lafayette radio station Elton John sings *Sail Away to Innocence.* Here and there, dilapidated barns look like ships being built, their skeletal frameworks waiting to be fleshed out.

Outside Rensselaer, Indiana -- across the busy highway from a McDonald's -- an abandoned seventy-four-acre farm is for sale. Like me, like many, it has outlived its original purpose and must find new meaning; grown up and gone are the children who once accompanied me on visits to their grandparents' house.

Skirting Chicago, I finally reach Wisconsin with its welcoming sign of yellow letters painted on brown logs. "Feel the bump? That's the state line," my father teased more than forty years ago, and so I teased my children twenty years later.

Time for supper: Heading east toward Lake Michigan and my old home, I feel as if I'm just getting back after a day at Hannans' farm or a journey to my mother's childhood. No tapes could have shared such intimate stories. No plane could have flown so far.

The Milk Pitcher

Simple things -- even a milk pitcher -- can become significant, making us feel more at home in the spinning universe.

When I was a toddler, the whole world appeared magical. Had a pitcher leapt from the table and zoomed about the room, I would have thought it normal. But my sisters, older by three and six years, had lived long enough to know there was a certain underlying order -- the sun rose, the sun set, and my serene, predictable mother never got upset.

One day, seated in my highchair by the table, I saw one sister accidentally drop her glass of milk. Mom scrambled to clean up the mess. Next, my other sister knocked over a glass, which shattered on the floor. Mom cleaned up that even messier mess.

Finally, I entered the scene -- throwing my cup of milk to the floor and smiling in triumph.

The room, my sisters say, fell silent as my mother picked up the pitcher and -- calmly and serenely -- poured the remaining milk all over the table, even shaking out the last few drops before setting it back down.

Year after year, meal after meal, the ample pewter pitcher sat on our table. No one recalls exactly when it entered our lives, but it was always there, a silent sentinel to our daily communion. Unlike the glassware and dishes that disappeared through the years by slipping from our hands, this alone remains from the childhood kitchen. By the time I'd grown up, it was battered and blackened with age -- crooked lip and all -- from the use and abuse we children had given it.

A pitcher of plenty to quench our thirst, most of all it held meaning. Like the fairy-tale pitcher that never emptied, it poured endless love. It spoke of a mother who time and again was there for us -- meals at the ready, bread from the oven, snacks after school. A mom who, over and over, picked up the shattered pieces of our day and made us whole.

When I received a shiny pewter pitcher as a wedding gift, time flashed forward. Holding it in my hands, I thought of meals to come, future children grasping its handle, and my packing and unpacking it as we moved from apartment to apartment, house to house. What would we all be like when it turned old? And where would we be?

The "new" pitcher has aged more than a quarter of a century. Not as battered as its predecessor, it's getting there. For years now, it has occupied an Ohio kitchen. I remember how I agonized over the move to a new city and new house. "Don't worry," Mother said. "As soon as your favorite things are there, it'll feel more like home."

When I dug through the packing boxes and stumbled upon the friendly pewter pitcher, I knew exactly what she meant. It was as if I had unearthed hearth and home. Setting it on the shelf, I felt settled myself.

A few years ago, my son moved to an apartment in Boston. Later, I went to visit. As he put the key into the lock, the door swung open, revealing the kitchen. Against the wall was a table holding a small white ceramic pitcher. I hadn't seen or thought of it in years, but there it was -- with the comical cow painted on its surface. It was a perfect size for a young child. Every morning, long ago, I had placed it in front of him at breakfast.

"I like seeing it when I first come in the door," he said with a shy smile, as if I didn't understand. "It feels like home."

After all these years, the world can still spill some magic.

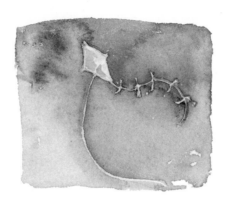

Kite Flying

I don't know when and where my father mastered the art of kite flying. Perhaps his birth in the windy month of March made him a natural. Raised by an uncle, who was a busy grocer, Dad probably acquired his skill through trial and error. I imagine him high on a blustery bluff in Eau Claire, Wisconsin, letting out the line just so, plucking the string like a violin, until his fingers talked with the tugging sail above.

I first watched him fly a kite on a sand dune overlooking Lake Michigan. Awaiting our turn, we children would roll down the hill, then rush back to his side, only to abandon him again and again for the downhill thrill. The biggest pleasure in that pre-television era, however, was the kite outing itself -- the togetherness.

Had I lingered next to him, I might have learned the technique that made our kites fly higher and stay up longer than all the other ones we saw. How had Dad known -- back home at his workbench (before kites came ready to assemble) -- where to join the spine and bow sticks? Where to anchor the string bridle? And, from raggedy strips of old sheets, how long to make the tail?

What I remember best from our sandy launching site is the sound of wind yanking a framework of rustling tissue upward amidst our shouts. And the fluttering of waves and whitecaps, of hair across eyes, of Windbreakers that never stayed shut, of the kite's long tail on its skyward journey. Staying up for so long, the kite gave us more than a reading of wind and weather. It told of a father who never gave up, who went the distance, who knew -- when the kite started to dip toward the horizon -- how to right it.

Carrying our paper shield back home, we felt like crusaders -- or soldiers carrying our colors back from battle. On windless days, the kite, hanging on a hook in the garage, wilted as it awaited the next outing. In flight, it came alive; sometimes, it broke free, traveling to where we could only dream to be.

Years later, I grew up, traveling almost as far. When my firstborn arrived, I hung a decorative, stained-glass kite in his nursery window. "Kite" was one of the first words he learned to say. Kite flying was one of the first activities I planned to share.

By that time, kites came in all shapes and sizes, precut in prefab packaging. There was no working together in a huddle over a workbench. What could be better or easier? I foolishly thought.

I remember a field behind Highland School. And a son and later a daughter dashing about like the wind in my ears. And scarves flapping and the kite shuddering in our hands before we let go.

Again and again, it veered about, dipped and thudded to the ground, without ever setting sail. What had been bliss in my childhood became a study of frustration in my adulthood. And in my children's lives. Now grown, they no doubt avert their eyes when they see a kite in a store window, remembering failed afternoons.

Why didn't I stay with it? Or find someone who would show us how? I could have given my children an example of stick-to-itiveness and follow-through and learning-from-failure. We should have made more of our own spontaneous fun, instead of relying on television and lessons after school and shopping malls.

Windy days won't wait forever.

Comfort comes in the thought of future grandchildren. If I start now to hone my skills, some March day, when my son or daughter is too busy to entertain a restless toddler or two, I can take the children high up on a hill. Then, when my kite snaps with life in the sunlight, I will assure them: "You come from a long line of kite flyers. Someday, you will do this, too -- like your great-grandfather before you."

May Baskets

Does newborn May still arrive in a basket at the door? As children, we helped usher her in. We never danced around a Maypole, much less saw one. We never heard of Flora, the Roman goddess of springtime, nor of how people used to gather flowers in her honor. But we sensed what must be done.

May First called for a celebration. It was up to us to throw one. Older siblings, in those pre-television days, initiated me in a ritual that had been handed down from one generation to another. How else could the vestige of an English habit have reached the hinterland of a Midwestern state?

When my two sisters explained that a basket was basic for this rite, I understood. Like primitive man and woman, my young self yearned to make one. But, unlike those forebears, who used grass, palm leaves, birch bark or willow, we wove our baskets from strips of colored construction paper.

Besides flowers, our latticed containers cradled meaning. Hadn't baby Moses floated down the Nile in a reed basket? Weren't bassinets for newborns? Easter baskets for eggs? Ours, too, would celebrate new life -- *spring.*

The picking was plentiful in the woods behind our house: violets, lilies of the valley, and bloodroot with its showy white bloom.

Most spectacular was swamp marigold, aglow along a creek. My oldest sister had christened the area "Nature," claiming it as her own. She carved two walking sticks for her best friend and herself and whittled the name in each. The place, she said, was secret. Each time she led me there, she made me close my eyes. But when I opened them in the nursery of the year, I saw small, puffy mounds of yellow flowers, like footstools in cold mud.

"The blossoms were like buttercups," she remembers. "The most beautiful part was picking them and putting them in our baskets. They wilted fast, so I don't know if they were still pretty after the people got them."

That was the trick. In order to deliver May baskets, you had to plan ahead. You had to have your baskets made beforehand, all lined up, ready to go.

That morning you rose before dawn and picked flowers in the gray light. You brought along a water-filled Mason jar or a bucket, or both, with the help of a wagon, which you pulled just so far and then left by the edge of the wood or at the top of the bank. Afterward, racing home, you filled the baskets and sped them to the waking houses of friends and neighbors, so the first thing they saw when they left for school or work was your May basket.

To do it later in the day was bad form, bad luck. But that was better than not doing it at all.

The basket's handle, my sister recalls, was the tricky part. "It was destined for the doorknob but was flimsy and sometimes fell off."

When that happened, we'd find a different place to leave it. Then we'd duck behind nearby bushes to await its discovery and gauge the reaction. If the suspense grew too great, we'd ring the doorbell -- and jump back to our hiding place or sprint across the yard.

That was the fun of May baskets, even more fun than Easter baskets -- making them, delivering them and running off without being seen.

My mother recalls picking blue windflowers and shooting stars on her grandmother's hill. My daughter remembers wrapping wet paper towels around the stems of flowers, then tinfoil, and finally a piece of construction paper in the shape of a cone.

Sometimes I like to think my mother still searches for flowers on my great-grandmother's hill; that my sisters and I -- with all of May, all of our lives before us -- still crouch low waiting for our baskets to be discovered; that my daughter at dawn still darts through silent green lawns.

Has the custom disappeared like our childhoods? Like the Maypole? Or does the month of May still arrive in a basket at the door?

Berry Picking

"Siblings will bond if only you parents would get out of their way," the child psychologist told his audience.

Though I was a young mother at the time, I realized he was right. All I had to do was recall my own childhood. Fluttering under our parental spotlight, my siblings and I vied for attention. With a mother and father at the ready, we relied less on one another. So it was mainly outside our parents' presence that we forged our friendship.

Karen is my oldest sister. Most of the time her life eluded mine, like her prized bag of marbles hanging out of my reach in the closet. Yet, sometimes she and I scaled the six-year wall that separated our worlds and created an island.

She balanced me on her bike's handlebars. She showed me how to hold a baseball bat and how to whittle a duck out of Ivory soap. Again and again, she carved her way into my heart. Part Wendy, part Peter Pan, she was a fearless tomboy -- throwing herself over home plate, building treehouses in the woods, grabbing a horse's mane and galloping off without saddle or bridle.

Once, a carousing crew of sailors visited our new baby sitter. My oldest sister secretly phoned the neighbors, woke my other sister and me, sneaked us into her bedroom and stood there behind the closed door -- clutching a baseball bat -- until help arrived.

Throughout my childhood, I clung to her like a caterpillar. Yet, of all the zillion starry moments, my first recollection of her shines brightest -- the day the bond formed.

Before dawn one summer morning, she tiptoed into the bedroom.

"Shhh," she whispered to four-year-old me and my seven-year-old sister, Sonja. "Don't wake up Mom and Dad."

"Why?"

"So we can surprise them and pick blackberries for breakfast."

As she helped me crawl inside my overalls -- "You can't wear shorts," she said; "the thorns will scratch your legs" -- I marveled at how easily her hands buttoned my straps and buckled my sandals while I stood on the bed. Why, she could dress me just like a mom -- and lift me, too.

Placing me on the floor, she put a belt around my waist. But first she threaded one end of it through the handle of a small tin bucket.

"That's for berries," she said, giving it a shake.

Like a uniform, it made me feel included. For the first time, I was going on an adventure with the big kids, instead of being left behind.

In soft, gray light, she led us tiptoeing down the stairs, showing us which creaky steps to miss, and into the kitchen, where she left a note for our parents. Then she guided us out the back door and down the street into the wider world -- from sidewalk to narrow path to no path at all. As my cocoon slipped away, I didn't look back.

Trooping along -- past creek, through prairie -- I realized what fun it was to be together, on our own. A parent would have made us eat breakfast first or brush our teeth or wait until it was light.

We stopped at a thorny thicket where plump blackberries tumbled everywhere. "Pick the ones along the edge," Karen warned, "so you don't get hurt." Like greedy bears, we helped ourselves to sweet fruit, filling our mouths as much as our pails.

I remember wishing I could always live there, in that spot, with my oldest sister. Though I knew nothing of the Potawatomi Indians who once had padded across the same undergrowth, I felt more wild than the civilized self I was being raised to be, more at home than in my house. There were no tables and chairs, no spoons or bowls. We could stoop down and pick our own breakfast and eat with our hands.

Deep in work, we hadn't noticed the sun swimming higher or our parents moving closer. Our dad's whistle gave them away. "Here we are," we shouted, happy to see them and share our bounty.

But I was sad, too. After they arrived, everything was different. The day changed, and the mood changed as we resumed our family roles.

We found a butterfly on our way home, and I wondered how it felt when we put it inside a jar. Hour after hour it tried to scale the walls of its glass house. Finally, I could stand it no longer. That evening I carried it outside, unscrewed the lid and shook it free -- just as my sister had done for me.

The Fourth of July

By the Fourth of July, we were knee-deep in summer. Enough time between the end of one school year and the start of another convinced us that such bliss would last forever. Happily, we wallowed in blue-sky days and firefly nights.

But, if summer was something we waded through, her sounds, lapping all around, are what I remember most: the fizz when ice cream hits root beer, the crack of a watermelon as it's sliced open, the squirt of the sprinkler and the squeak, squeak of a porch swing competing with crickets.

Waking up in the morning, I heard doves cooing on the eaves trough. At night, I fell asleep to the rhythmic sound of the deep foghorn and a lone train whistle off in the distance. Though they were present throughout all the seasons, I heard them best in summer.

Only in summer, as I drifted off to sleep, could I hear the crowd's cheers and the announcer's voice for a league of our own -- the Kenosha (Wisconsin) Comets. As the women in their tunics played hardball, I lay awake plotting ways to persuade my dad to take us to the next night's game.

Summer sounds played best of all on the Fourth. We'd rocket out of bed, aching with Christmas Eve impatience for the fireworks to begin. Parades and picnics helped pass the time. But nothing compared to the deafening display at the end of the day.

After breakfast, like the Potawatomi Indians who once roamed the woods behind our house, we would sense the earth's vibrations. Dropping to our knees, ears to the ground, we felt the drums, tubas, trumpets and trombones even before we heard them. "Come on, we'll be late," we shouted to our parents, and, cocker spaniel and all, we jumped into the car and sped to Library Park.

Sitting on the curb, cherry Popsicles in hand, my older sister Sonja and I stared as our oldest sister marched by, carrying the American flag for her Girl Scout troop. Though the band played a rousing John Philip Sousa piece, we watched in stunned silence. Would we ever be that old, that big, that competent? We'd just sat across from her at breakfast eating our Cheerios, yet now she loomed larger than life, a celebrity.

By noontime, in our swimsuits, we three were on more equal footing at the shore of the lake. Under low limbs, with the snap of flags and beach towels nearby, the shout of voices rising from the water as a beach ball drifted toward the horizon, we helped our mother pour lemonade and pass her potato salad.

By late afternoon, fresh from showers and dressed in a combination of red, white and blue, we children disappeared with cap pistol ammunition and hammers to pound away on a secluded piece of cement until our dad's voice, rising above the din, called us home for supper.

That evening, on a stretch of park overlooking the lake,

we'd spread out our endless blanket, lie back and watch the stars come out one by one. "Tell us, again, Mother, how you got lost on the Fourth," we pleaded, our weary bodies grateful for the pause. The ritual of her story made time go faster, the fireworks start sooner.

"We always went to Fireman's Park," she began softly. "It was huge, with a bandstand, dance hall, baseball field, merry-go-round and carnival booths."

She recalled new dresses made just for the Fourth, picnic baskets offering fried chicken and chocolate cake, and how once, in the dark, she was separated from her family.

"I started to cry," she remembered. "People talked to me, but they weren't people I wanted to talk to. I wanted to find my family. After a long time my father suddenly appeared. He scooped up my three-year-old self. There, in his arm, was something he'd won at a booth: a little bear whose eyes lit up when you pushed a button. Such heaven -- to be rescued by my father and given a toy."

After all these years, the sound of her voice in the hushed, expectant darkness is what I remember most -- more than all the booms that later shook the sky.

Lemon Sponge Cake

A cake can tell a lot about love. My father always said the best one he ever ate was made by Auntie Karen, who raised him after he was orphaned at age six. That he named his firstborn after her says how he felt about the woman. That he never ate a better cake says what he thought of her recipe. Unfortunately she never wrote it down.

That didn't stop my mother from trying to duplicate the lemon sponge cake. Every time Mom discovered a recipe, she'd try it -- proffering the finished product to my dad. The ritual never changed. We'd gather around the table, holding our breath, hoping this one would finally hit the mark. After savoring the first bite, he'd smile at my mother, wink and say, "Almost, but not quite." We kids exhaled, deflated.

Only after his eighty-fifth birthday did I realize what this has been all about. Though a stroke had robbed him of speech, it didn't stop him from offering an opinion about his annual cake: Holding thumb and index finger a fraction of an inch apart, he smiled and winked.

I suppose that if any one of those cakes had been served in his boyhood kitchen, with a dollop of nostalgia and Auntie Karen doting over him, it would have matched the original.

But why should he have told the truth and interrupted a good thing -- which produced a fifty-six-year parade of sponge cakes?

I probably would have given up long ago or told him to go bake one himself. But I think my mother figured it out more than half a century ago and just kept playing along -- an intimate, loving joke between the two.

My mother had her own favorite childhood cake. Her mother baked it for her every year on her birthday during threshing season, when neighbors came to help my grandfather at Deer Knoll Farm. That meant days when my grandmother fed twenty or more helpers and kept up with her chores and her four children.

Each noon was like Thanksgiving, with bowls of mashed potatoes and vegetables and huge platters of meat. Yet, on August 9, between cleaning up and starting supper, Grandmother would give a party for my mother.

With the air heavy from the threshing, friends walked down the dusty road from their farms. Grandmother set up a card table on the front lawn under low limbs. "She served us lemonade and made everything special," remembers my mother.

"The high point was the angel food cake, because it was baked just for me. She mashed my favorite black raspberries into the whipped cream, creating a luscious pink color. Then she slathered the cake with it. In the center, she always placed a bouquet of sweet peas, surrounded by pink candles."

My mother used to make me cakes, too. But what did I

23

know about love in my half-baked youth? One March birthday, when I was five, I had an angel food cake, frosted with pink-tinted whipped cream. It echoed no note in memory's music -- just another homemade cake. And I didn't like cake. Or food, for that matter. Except ice cream. Besides, I was more interested in presents.

When my world expanded into attending other children's parties, I saw store-bought cakes with filigrees of frosting, intricate roses and the birthday child's very own name inscribed across the top. The best was the one I coveted at Ginny Vincent's party: a circus cake, complete with plastic animals prancing in a ring under a striped canopy. Now, that was a cake! I hurried home and announced to my mother that at my next birthday I didn't want a plain cake but a fancy one like Ginny's.

The following March I got my wish. And, happily, every birthday thereafter, a store-bought cake.

Years later I heard the story of Deer Knoll Farm. And black raspberries and cold whipped cream on angel food cake. It mingled with the memory of my own long-ago party, giving the music a fuller, richer tone.

I thought of Auntie Karen. My grandmother. And, most of all, my mother. In their baking, all three had given a gift of themselves.

And my mother has proved, whether trying to duplicate a cake for her husband or giving a store-bought one to her daughter, she always knows the right recipe. By heart.

Summer's Bookends

Like green bookends on the year's shelf, the Memorial Day and Labor Day watermelons held summer in place. In between were lots of others, but none was more delicious than the first or as bittersweet as the last.

There used to be a season -- before back-to-school clothes arrived in July, before holiday decorations trimmed stores in September -- when watermelons had meaning.

The ritual took root during my parents' youth. After enduring the blizzards and bleakness of Wisconsin winters, they'd finally break through to bliss: hot summers and cold watermelon. There's something to be said for the "earned" moment -- when one must wait for things; when sweetness, or summer, is all the sweeter for its absence on either side.

And there's something to be said for knowing where produce grows. Florida? South America? My mother knew.

"Jefferson County watermelons," she said emphatically,

"were the best. Something about the soil. Take those from Columbia County, where Portage is. Why, they weren't fit to eat -- too pale, too many seeds and no flavor."

Jefferson County's were so clearly superior that her father would leave their farm in Dane County, drive to neighboring Jefferson County and "load up the back seat of his Nash, clear to the ceiling, with watermelons." He'd store them in the barn's cold-water tank, fishing them out for threshing parties and barn dances.

"They were huge," she recalled. "One was enough for the whole choir." After practice, on the church lawn, her dad, the choir director, would carve one into thirty pieces.

"We didn't have plates or forks or napkins. We'd just eat it with the juice running down. So cold and delicious -- I've never had one like it since."

For my dad, watermelon meant not only a summer rite but also a rite of passage. With the first money he earned as a newspaper boy, he bought one as a surprise for his family. Years later he recalled how proud he'd felt carrying it home on his bicycle.

My sisters and I didn't have to wait part of the summer for a crop to ripen. As each May 30 rolled around, neighborhood grocers, thanks to trucks pulling up from the South, stockpiled the fruit. With Christmas-tree-buying excitement, we'd dance around Dad until he drove us to Augie's Market.

While we kids scurried about, hugging a watermelon here, sitting on another there, he'd solemnly rap their green surfaces with his knuckle. Head lowered, ear cocked, he listened for the sound he'd been taught to recognize by his Uncle Alan, a grocer. Though I never stood still long enough to acquire the skill, Dad could tell, by such a tap, which ones were perfect.

"Sounds good, Augie," he'd say at last. "We'll take it."

Suddenly it was summer, as my father hoisted the watermelon onto his shoulder.

Tasting it in the back yard was like biting into a breeze. The melon's coldness cooled our faces. We felt like the big kids as we spit black seeds onto barefoot-warm grass.

Come Labor Day weekend, driving down a country lane, passing a roadside stand, my mother, with a memory of Jefferson County, would step on the brake and send us back to pick out a melon. Later, under the porch's awning, we'd try prolonging supper and the summer, while a whiff of fall made us feel the planet in its turning.

The jet age makes watermelon more available but perhaps less appreciated. Like fresh strawberries -- once jewels in summer's crown but now adornments for all the seasons -- watermelon can be bought almost year-round, even at Christmas. Quartered, or as a slice served on Styrofoam under plastic wrap, it rarely comes home on a shoulder -- or piled high in a car.

Just when I thought watermelon had lost its magic, and summer was about to tumble from the shelf, Susie, a six-year-old who lives across the street from where I grew up, proved me wrong. Pulling back large leaves in her very own garden, she revealed a pair of baby watermelons. The moment was better than Jefferson County, better than Augie's, and it was right in my old neighborhood.

Apple Picking

When I see apples, ripe and heavy, bend a bough low, I remember the first time I picked them. That was long ago, a year when late summer's warmth lingered into fall. But winter, I knew, was on the way, because my sister's horse had begun to grow her thick brown coat.

Sometimes my sister Karen, six years my senior, took me for rides on Glory. One day, as I sat behind Karen, we trotted off bareback toward the open fields. When her horse's gait quickened to a canter, then a gallop, my arms tightened all the more around Karen's waist. I rested my head against her back, keeping my eyes closed -- the better to quiet my fears and hear the rhythmic roll of hoofs, the whistle of wind.

When we stopped near a wood lot, trees, poised like dancers, invited us in. Beneath their armlike branches, the horse stepped cautiously, head lowered. We followed her example, flattening ourselves along the line of her neck. Jonathans and McIntoshes and other reds passed in review until we came to a tree of green.

Guiding Glory to a stop under its low-slung branches, my sister picked a glistening apple and passed it back to me. I placed it and another and another on my lap, making a sling out of my sweat shirt. When the makeshift basket could bear no more, we each reached up, selecting an apple. I polished mine shiny on my shirt and took a bite. Though it was noon, the night's tart chill was still trapped inside the fruit. Not before or since has an apple tasted that good.

I don't recall going back to pick apples again -- not from high on a horse's back, sheltered by my big sister. Later that fall my father contracted tuberculosis. Life was pared to essentials. Certainly, for city dwellers, a horse was a frivolous expense. By winter, when her coat had completely grown, Glory was sold.

Once, when our children were small, my husband and I piled them into the station wagon and drove to an orchard on the outskirts of town. A farmer's ladder and our obliging arms elevated them to leafy heights. They plucked away, turning over their bounty to us below, saying, "Wait 'til you see this" and "You won't believe" and "Wow, here's a winner."

We filled two bushel baskets that warm Saturday afternoon. Afterward, I spread a cloth at the base of a venerable tree, where we picnicked in the midst of plenty.

Propping the camera on a fence, we pressed the time-release button and preserved the moment. The family portrait, frozen in time, is full of smiles -- as if we'd always be together, year after year, reaping the harvest.

Life intervened. I don't recall going back to pick apples again. Other falls found us driving down gravel country roads to buy a bushel of apples here, a pumpkin there. Always the lessons after school. Field hockey games on Saturdays. Errands.

But the experience must have meant something to my daughter. Ever since, she has kept the family photo from that day hanging on a wall in her room. One fall, before leaving for her junior year at college, she suggested, "Let's go apple picking."

Life intervened. There were jobs to do. Appointments to keep. Errands.

A week later, after saying goodbye outside her dormitory, I watched her become smaller and smaller -- child-size -- in the car's rearview mirror. Suddenly it struck me: We hadn't gone apple picking.

Even if we had, could we have gone back to those times we both had tasted -- when the world, like a plentiful orchard, stood poised and promising?

The Bogeyman

As a child, I was afraid of many things -- fluttering moths, slithering snakes and, most of all, the bogeyman.

"Can I play?" I'd beg my older sisters and their friends.

"No, and if you try to follow us, the bogeyman will get you."

Time and again, I'd run shrieking to the safety of our back yard.

"There's no such thing as a bogeyman," my mother tried to assure me. But how could she know? She stayed mainly in the house. She didn't play up and down the block like the big kids. All I knew was, I was afraid and couldn't act otherwise.

It's easy to be ourselves when we're children. Like babies staring unself-consciously, we live openly. We are what we are -- hungry or sleepy, happy or angry, loving or afraid. We cannot be something we are not, and perhaps this inspires our childhood fascination with costumes. A disguise quickly transforms us into prince or princess, Zorro or zebra, ghost or witch.

One long-ago Halloween, dressed as the Queen of Hearts, I set off into the dusk, tagging after my sisters and their friends. My face grew warm and moist behind my mask, a bulky jacket hid most of my costume, and my long skirt made navigating awkward. Still, I managed to feel regal.

With open sacks we raced from house to house, up one side of the block, down the other, barely pausing to say thank you. Our beggars' bags grew heavier as the moonless night closed in.

We came to a house all dark and dreary, a house we usually didn't notice, as it lacked the light of children. In the front yard, a birch tree's branches creaked like chalk against the blackboard sky.

"Why are we stopping?" I asked, feeling uncertain, as we climbed some steps.

"Because," the big kids whispered in unison, and someone rang the doorbell.

Though I was only five, I knew our reason: greed.

A wan-looking man opened the door.

"Wait here," he said. "I'll be right back. Now don't go away, because I'm gonna get a real nice treat."

What could it be? we wondered aloud. Seconds passed. Minutes. Must be special, we told ourselves, because he was taking so long. We huddled together on the front porch. Standing on tiptoe I strained to see over the big kids' shoulders.

Then, when we thought he'd never return, from behind us there came an unearthly hiss, a howling roar. Wheeling about and looking up, I was first in line in front of a looming green monster. With bobbing head and flailing arms, it lurched toward me.

Dropping our candy, my sisters ran one way and I ran the

other -- straight home and into my mother's lap.

"There is, too, a bogeyman," I told her when I finally found my voice.

I still believe it today, except that when we're adults the monster often lurks within, making us afraid of becoming all that we are meant to be. The scariest thing about masks and disguises isn't putting them on, it's peeling them off -- one by one -- and revealing who we really are.

November Winds

November winds prune trees, scattering leaves. Birds, wedging south, skim the sky. Every year I, too, fly -- down a long corridor of Thanksgivings past.

Hurrying back to 1950, I enter a land devoid of TV dinners or turbo bread machines, microwave meals or fast-food restaurants. It was a time when supper was served as regularly as a clock strikes six. A time when everyone sat down together.

My mother, who had few conveniences, had less time and spent more of it canning and baking. I can still sense the warm aroma of her homemade pies and breads as I wake up once more on that morning long ago. On the bedroom windowsill is a little stack of snow, like a white invitation, announcing the holidays.

Laughter from below makes me wonder what I'm missing, and I scurry downstairs. Our kitchen swims with relatives and the dizzying scent of roasting turkey. After breakfast, we kids help set the stage -- bringing in firewood, pulling up a mix of chairs to the dining-room table.

When Dad leaves to make hospital rounds, I tag along. Driving on our deserted street, we pass the houses of neighbors "safely gathered in." Downtown is eerily silent, too, but offers a bigger surprise: Christmas decorations hanging from the street lights. I scrunch low, almost to the floorboards, to better see the striped candy canes swaying overhead.

Thanksgiving -- and Christmas on the way. The excitement is overwhelming, like the roar of the old 400 arriving from Minneapolis with Aunt Alma. We meet her train on the way home from the hospital. I bury my cold face in the fur of her coat. In the car, I sit next to her so I can play with her jingling gold charm bracelet.

Later, after prayers of thanksgiving, we devour in minutes what it took Mother days to prepare. I fill up on a drumstick -- and mountains of mashed potatoes swimming in gravy, apple pie and ice cream, and chocolates from the Whitman's Sampler. When we kids can eat no more, we stretch out on the floor to recover.

Later, I roll onto my stomach to color by the fireplace. The firelight and even the orange glow from the radio's dial cast a magic spell.

I linger too long. I want to revisit Thanksgiving thirteen years later, when I was a junior in college, home for the holiday. Pushing open the door, I hear a television's relentless replaying of Monday's funeral -- the muffled drumbeat, the creaking of the caisson. Someday these scenes will be etched across our collective memory. In 1963, they are raw and riveting.

As a nation, we mourn.

I close the door and tiptoe away. Walking past another thirteen years, I find the entrance to 1976 and peek inside. My five-year-old daughter wears a white paper Pilgrim's hat and sings *Over the River and Thro' the Woods*, which she practiced all the way to Grandmother's house -- past Ohio fields, past Wisconsin fences.

Her expectations are high. Trying to sing as perfectly as she did at school, she falters -- in front of aunts and uncles, grandparents and cousins -- and weeps in my lap. Her relatives, however, applaud her efforts, showing what family is all about. They're there to catch us when we fall.

Her spirits lift when she joins her cousins in living-room gymnastics. That evening, after our traditional game of charades, they sleep through the night in front of the fireplace.

Thank goodness for Thanksgiving. Lacking commercialism, it reminds us of what is truly important -- like the insight Mother shared standing at this year's threshold:

"After the Depression, after we lost the farm, I thought I had nothing. In reality, I had everything -- my parents, my school, my friends. And I wasn't hungry. What a gift to be able to have all that. The riches in the world are in the people you love."

November winds may prune and scatter. But Thanksgiving brings us together.

Billy the Brownie

Long ago, when I was my elfin self, I fell in love with a brownie. Every day after school, between Thanksgiving and Christmas, I'd rush home to listen to *The Adventures of Billy the Brownie* on radio.

Waiting for dusk and the start of the five o'clock show was like waiting for Christmas. The fifteen-minute program was pure magic. With blue twilight trapped outside our living-room windows, my sister Sonja and I sat in front of the merry Magnavox, transported.

The show was sponsored by Schuster's, a Milwaukee department store; yet, I figured that every child in America was listening, not just those of us living close enough to WTMJ's signal.

Billy the Brownie, Santa's chief elf, arrived ahead of time to help us children get ready. He and Larry Teich -- the show's host and creator -- urged us to write letters to Santa at the North Pole. Every day, as they selected some to read, I waited for Billy to read mine. He never did. Yet, that did not stop me from writing each year and dropping my letter into a cold mailbox with my mittened hand.

Thanks to the miracle of long-distance telephone calls, there was always a North Pole update. Breathlessly, we'd listen in as Billy and Larry interviewed Santa and his brownies, who were busily making our toys -- such as a little tea set and the doll's wardrobe trunk I wanted. Best of all, we'd hear Santa's own progress reports after he started his long trip across the sky -- how Dasher was doing or whether needed repairs to the sleigh were causing a delay. Would Santa make it by Christmas Eve? Wallowing in delicious agony, we hung on until the next cliff-hanging episode.

Meanwhile, Mother bustled in the background, a tiptoeing here, a rustle of packages there. Mingled in memory is the scent of cardamom as she carried her homemade Norwegian cookies to the cold attic, where they would stay fresh until their unveiling Christmas Eve.

But how could I notice Mother when I was listening to magic -- a story from *The Magic Christmas Book*, which opened only when all of us in radio land would face the lighted dial and say, "I have been good." We had to mean it -- or else, on some dreaded days, the book's cover wouldn't squeak open for a story.

Then Billy and Larry conferred, saying whoever was to blame knew why -- and I, with countless others, squirmed in guilt, vowing to be better.

In 1955, the show -- after a twenty-five-year run -- went off the air. By then I was twelve, way past my Billy the Brownie stage; yet, sometimes, if I saw something dart by a winter window, I'd wonder if it might be the little elf, dressed in brown, checking up on me.

Last December I ordered three tiny "tumbling elves" made out of felt.

Why would someone my age do such a thing? I asked my friend Jean Goldsmith as I showed her my purchase.

"Probably," she said, "because they remind you of Billy the Brownie."

"You knew Billy, too?" I asked, astounded. And we were off -- two Columbus, Ohio, women comparing notes about a childhood hero. Jean grew up in Milwaukee. She can still hear the jingle bell in Billy's cap, still remember worrying "right up to Christmas Eve if Santa would make it."

This December when she called her brother back in her hometown they teased each other about whose name was in Santa's "good" book: "He said his always was and mine was not."

Thanks to her thoughtful sister-in-law, Jean received a package a few days later from *The Milwaukee Journal*, filled with nostalgic clippings about Billy the Brownie.

"It's so exciting," she said, "like listening to the radio all over again."

I used to think that magic appeared only on my old radio -- or on a movie screen or in a land far, far away. Yet, life itself is the real miracle. It's family, and it's friends. Long ago, when I tried so hard to open Billy the Brownie's magic storybook, I didn't realize I was already living an enchanted tale: my parents creating Christmas; our family going to sleep, safe, under one roof, as stars and children awaited the timeless traveler.

I'd like to step back into the past and listen to Billy the Brownie and discover my presents under the tree. But first, on Christmas Eve, I'd like to climb one more time up to a frosty attic, following the scent of cardamom. Beneath the high pitch of a timbered ceiling, so much like the nave of a Norwegian church, I'd find nestled in tissue paper, in a large box, my mother's *fattigmanns bakkels* -- as sure a sign as the turning calendar that we all had arrived at another Christmas.

Now, that would be magic. Pure magic.

Christmas Bell

Can you hear the bell of a country church? Long ago -- before radio and television and rock music cluttered the air -- its deep, rich tone reached inside a heart. In that quieter time, before the farm hummed with electricity, homemade chocolates were kept cold under the snow, and candles flickered on the Christmas tree.

Never did the bell ring as sweetly as on Christmas Eve, echoing across prairie snow to call in my mother, then a young girl, from chores. All day, while stripping tobacco in the shed, she had yearned for the sound to set her free. Finally, at dusk, she heard it, resonating over still land, rolling out the holidays.

Rushing into the house, where smells of cinnamon and cardamom, turkey and sage swirled through the steaming kitchen, she quickly washed up and changed into her new dress. Then she waited -- and waited -- by the window. Would Grandmother Julia, walking up the lane in her long black skirt and cape, be carrying a package big enough to hold a doll?

40

I knew none of this Christmases later, when I was a young girl. I yearned to hear only jingling bells on Santa's sleigh. One Christmas Eve, when all the world was asleep, I strained in hushed darkness to hear the sound.

Instead, the doorbell chimed. Why, I wondered, would Santa arrive at our front door when we had a chimney? I scampered past my older sister asleep in the bed next to mine, past my oldest sister's room, and dropped to my knees to peek through the banister. A cold crush of air reached my toes as Father let in a mufflered man who carried a towering white object. As they disappeared into the living room, I crept downstairs.

"It's perfect," I heard Mother say.

"Remarkable," Father agreed.

"You took good care of me, Doc," the man said. "I want to repay. Here, I'll plug it in."

A magical sound filled the air, again and again. I could wait no longer; running in, I saw a church steeple as tall as I was. At its base, a carved figure pulled a rope back and forth, back and forth, ringing a silver bell in the belfry. I wanted to be small enough to climb inside and ring it, too.

Many years later -- after Christmas lights had been stored away but snow still glazed the ground -- I visited Boston. Hoping to hear the last bell cast by Paul Revere, I walked up Tremont Street one Sunday toward King's Chapel. Suddenly, above the jangle of traffic, the bell from 1816 awoke in the belfry. Each pull offered resounding proof why Revere had called it "the sweetest bell we ever made."

After services, the organist led me up flights of stairs into the tower room, where a rope dangled from the ceiling.

"Would you like to pull it?" she asked, surprising me. Remembering my long-ago Christmas wish, I tugged again and again -- rocking the flywheel, causing the clapper to strike the two-and-a-half tons of cast metal. Beyond the window and overhead, I heard the bell Revere had tuned reverberate once more.

"He came to supervise the installation himself," the organist said as she guided me up more flights under hand-hewn beams, past stone walls, until we emerged through a trapdoor into the belfry. There hung the mighty bell. Touching its cold surface, reading the inscription -- "Paul Revere, 1816" -- I felt the past and present come together.

Above, pigeons cooed and flapped their wings. Below, worshipers crisscrossed their way through snow. Suspended between sky and earth, I sensed a truth: Some gifts are unexpected -- such as being up later than one's older sisters and playing with a new toy first, or ringing a bell in Boston.

The most unexpected of all is a bell I never heard, from a time I never knew -- when my mother was a girl growing up on the prairie.

During Christmas services she would watch two men with water buckets stand near the candle-lighted spruce, just in case. In the loft, while her father led the choir and her mother sang carols, she cradled her new doll.

"Hush," she whispered to it at the close of church. "Hear the bell?"

Floating far above, one clear tone after another filled the frosty air.

Now, each Christmas Eve, the unexpected echo reaches me.

The Blue Sled

Blue: Juniper berries. Shadows on snow. A scarf of light as day skates toward night. For me, it's as much a color of Christmas as red and green. Now, over the white slope of memory slides a blue sleigh of yesterdays -- a time before Rollerblades, before streets were salted, when tires still wore chains.

Reaching in, I grab a brightly wrapped day before Christmas. My older sisters and I awoke that frosty morning to a jing, jing, jingle and "ho-ho-ho's." In the hall we discovered our father holding a harness of sleigh bells. We'd seen it before, but always on a hook in the garage. It used to belong to my father's Uncle Alan, who had raised him, and it was worn by the horse that pulled the sleigh from Uncle Alan's grocery.

Racing home from school on icy days, my father and his friends would grab the back of this delivery sleigh and "skate" over the streets. The driver, with his whip, tried to scare them off. But, if he noticed my dad, he'd stop and say,

"Oh, it's you, Leif. Climb aboard."

"Look outside," our father now said. Pressing our faces to the cold windowpane, we saw in real life what we'd heard only in song: a real, live horse hitched to a one-horse open sleigh. More eager than the pawing hoof, we jumped out of our pajamas into snowsuits and flew out the door.

Father put the bell harness on the shiny black horse, which puffed clouds of smoke like a small steam engine. "Climb aboard," Dad said, helping us in. Wedged between Mother and a sister, I sat in back under a woolly blanket. My oldest sister sat in front, beside Father, our driver. One flick of the reins, and we were off, skimming down one snowy street, jingling up another, delivering presents just like Santa.

Again, reaching into memory's sleigh, I push past days of toboggan rides, past sledding parties when snow caked in the necks of our mittens, and grasp a Christmas afternoon when the world grew quiet.

After presents were opened and the holiday dinner was finished, I found myself alone with my parents in the snowy woods behind our house. Long before I entered the world, Dad had fastened three pieces of wood to a sled, creating a little sleigh for my sister Karen, his firstborn.

Painting it the blue of a juniper berry, he finished it before her first snowfall.

When she outgrew it, Sonja, my next-oldest sister, inherited it. Now it was mine.

There I was, daughter number three -- dressed in hand-me-down clothes in a hand-me-down sled -- being pulled by my parents through deep snow. Like the blue tail of a comet, I trailed behind, hearing the crunch of their boots as they blazed a path through the universe. Smiling at each other, they smiled back at me as we traveled under the muted bell of silence. More spectacular than a jingling ride in a one-horse open sleigh, it was bliss. Just the three of us. And my parents' undivided attention.

Another day is left to relive -- one from January 1977. Shortly after Sonja died, Mother and I went to help my brother-in-law go through her things. Tucked at the back of a shelf, I discovered a small package wrapped in Christmas paper that she'd never sent.

The attached note bore my name, along with this message: "I know you said you'd be upset if anything happened to the blue sled. Yet even if it did, you have the memory of that time with Mom and Dad forever."

Opening the box, I found an ornament in the shape of our little homemade sleigh.

She was right. Though I recall no presents from that long-ago Christmas, I remember a moment in the white woods, a lasting gift. Which tells me most of all what to give the children. Our time. Someday it will be too late.

The Christmas Jar

What will happen to the presents your children made -- the cookbook holder or, for keeping out the cold, the "draft dodger"? When you take down the tree, where will you put the jingle-bell-pipe-cleaner ornament carried home from nursery school on a tiny wrist? Young eyes are watching.

Once I could have told you exactly how my hands felt as they tried to steady the brush. Painting the empty peanut-butter jar white was easy.

"After they dry, we'll paint the rims gold," my teacher said.

That was hard, applying the trim so that the gold -- a gold so gold it out-glittered the slanting sun against the snow -- wouldn't trickle down onto the white.

Carrying the jar home between mittens, I was bearing -- if not gold, frankincense and myrrh -- at least gold.

Hiding the tissue-wrapped present under my bed, I could hardly wait until my parents opened it on Christmas morning.

Their reaction didn't disappoint me.

For weeks, months, maybe years, I proudly looked upon my Christmas jar on a desk or windowsill.

One day I noticed it behind a cupboard's glass doors and later, behind its lower, wooden ones. Each new, remote site made me feel diminished. Yet, whenever I discovered the old gift, I unearthed a time capsule: Like a conch shell echoing the ocean, the jar held the sound of kids shouting on the playground, Mr. Perry pulling the school bell, Miss Weibel reading *The Boxcar Children*. It captured the scents of drying paint, thawing snowsuits in the cloakroom and Christmas greens.

You'd think, given my history, that I had prominently displayed every artifact my children made. I did post drawings, hang wind chimes, use pots to hold paper clips.

During the summer, packing up to move to a smaller house, I came across a mountain of their work, eventually saved for two decades, in the attic: pictures hammered out of copper, chalk drawings of pumpkins, yarn wreaths, even the "draft dodger" and cookbook holder. What do they contribute to a child's self-esteem while hidden in the dark?

Knowing I had to winnow these relics into a sizable mound, I devised a plan:

When I found something signed "T. Chapman" and couldn't recall whether Tyler or Tia had made it, I put it in a "discard box." When finally I left a box at the curb, I felt pangs of regret but a sense of accomplishment, too.

Undoubtedly, in a fit of housecleaning, my mother once happened across my old Christmas jar and discarded it. Had she asked, I would have said, "Everything else can be thrown away, but that's the one thing I care about."

In August, after cleaning my attic, I visited her. I knew that the jar had long since vanished, but I found myself peering into dark corners. Then the thought hit me: What if I'd thrown out a child's "Christmas jar" in trying to squeeze into a smaller house?

On a Toledo visit at Thanksgiving, I noticed a cardinal -- a hooked rug -- hanging above my mother-in-law's desk.

"I remember working on it really hard as Christmas came closer and closer," my twenty-five-year-old daughter recalled, "and realizing I wasn't going to get it done.

"You said I could give it to her and tell her I would finish it later.

"Looking at all those gaping, blank squares on the big plastic grid, I wondered if I ever would. . . . It was arduous at times. I remember breaking out in a sweat and running up to my room.

"Finally, there was that ultimate feeling of having the whole thing covered. I'd run my hands across it over and over and not feel a single empty space.

"It's amazing Grandma has kept it there all these years. . . . It's so shaggy-looking, but I remember thinking it looked just as good as any hooked rug anywhere."

"Is it the most favorite gift you ever gave as a child?" I asked, hoping she wouldn't mention something set by the curb.

"Oh, yes."

If we're lucky, the ones we save are the ones they love.

Fallow Fields

In the heart of winter, I must remember what I learned one summer long ago: Farmers do not berate a fallow field.

"Time to let it rest," Walt Hannan explained, as he and my six-year-old self tromped over the loose earth. "Next season we'll plant something here. Wait till you see how it grows."

He and I crossed the unfurrowed field until we reached one filled with muskmelons. Bending down, he took his knife and sliced open a ripe fruit, handing me a piece. It was warm to its center, like the sun above. Lots of things were warm at Hannans' farm: milk from the cow, eggs from under a hen, newborn kittens in the hayloft.

Time and again, trailing my big sister down dusty roads, I entered this foreign land, leaving behind our mowed and clipped civilization. For whenever she went to ride her horse, boarded at Hannans' farm, I tagged along. Taking two buses to the end of the line, we walked the remaining mile. Close-knit houses slipped away, as field upon field filled in the view. Just when my small legs could bear no more, the barn's roof loomed ahead, making me race the rest of the way.

And so it was, playing by myself during the long hours my sister rode and rode and rode, I became acquainted with different rhythms, recurring cycles. One had to learn patience waiting for a sister to return from her endless ride; waiting for a crop of corn, planted in spring, to reach fruition and finally be sold. Patience, from the haying to the stacking of bales in a barn's loft, from fallow to full.

Yet sometimes, after honest labor, after cultivating the soil and planting a crop, after months of waiting, there was nothing to reap. Too much rain. Too little. Each would take its toll. Or insects. Or blight. Life, I learned, could be hard. Unpredictable.

Walt Hannan and his wife, Mary, had no children. They were good, kind people who often let my sister and me put our feet under their table. I remember going into their back room to wash up, the screen door smacking shut behind me, and smelling the close, overwhelming fragrance of harvested muskmelons heaped in mounds on the floor.

The table held a still life of vegetables I had helped pull from Mary's garden -- and roasted chicken they hadn't bought at the store. Not far outside their back door was a stump. The first time I realized its purpose, it was raining. Alarmed when I saw a chicken held down, the hatchet held high, I told Walt to stop.

"Don't worry," he said. "It doesn't hurt them when it's raining." How I ached to believe him.

My sister and I often stayed overnight in the upstairs spare bedroom. Sometimes the Hannans even let us sleep in the hayloft. On such a night, when summer slipped into autumn, we heard the wind rustling dry corn stalks. It told us, before other city folk, that winter was on its way.

Even then the farm drew us. While my sister trotted her

horse across frozen ground, I ice-skated. Afterward, we warmed ourselves over the furnace grate on the living-room floor, dancing about when our stocking feet could no longer bear the heat.

Wet pastures and mud and the promise on the wind of apple blossoms told us life was returning to the farm, even before we saw the baby chicks or newborn foal.

That was long ago. The farm and those who lived there have vanished, like a dream, like childhood. A subdivision claims what then was country -- the fields not only fallow but forgotten.

Still, on this winter day, one can remember their lesson: If there is no sense of hope or personal growth, be patient. We may be resting, replenishing our own inner soil. For, just as day follows night and darkness light, something will take root. And round itself into life.

Miss Learn

Though the Koshkonong Prairie still exists near Madison, Wisconsin, its Carpenter School, a one-room schoolhouse, now dwells in the landscape of memory.

On a February day, when temperatures drop and the snow swirls outside, you can still hear the far-off jingle of bells coming closer and closer. In sleighs filled with sweet-smelling hay and warm buffalo robes, the fathers, frozen in time, arrive to take the children home.

"Every Valentine's Day, we had a large box festooned with pink and red crepe paper into which we dropped our homemade valentines for our schoolmates," my mother, at seventy-six, recalls. "I always worried, 'What if I don't get any?' But of course I did. And I read them over and over again. I treasured them."

A graduate of the University of Wisconsin, she grew up on the prairie on her family's farm. With wondrous sunsets and wildflowers and a pony of her own, she loved it all. "But most of all, I loved Carpenter School and Miss

Susannah Learn, my teacher for eight grades."

"Learn" -- a remarkable name for an educator. But even more remarkable was the teacher herself. Who wouldn't love someone who keeps you after school for whispering, then offers you kind words of encouragement with a dish of chocolate pudding? Wearing a pretty dress, made by her own hands and decorated with touches of tatting, Miss Learn stands in the doorway of the one-room schoolhouse. She waves goodbye to the happy little girl who dances off toward home.

Remembering that moment of sweet discipline delivered by her teacher so long ago, my mother smiles. "Miss Learn was a jewel. Beautiful and remarkable."

Miss Learn had been hired by my mother's father, a farmer and president of the local school board. "Get all the education you can," he used to tell his daughter. "It's the only thing people can't take away from you." Since part of her pay was room and board, Miss Learn took turns living with the families of her students, including my mother's.

During one such time, when my mother was only four years old, she stood at the window and cried as she watched her older siblings and Miss Learn leave for school. "Let her come," said Miss Learn to my grandmother. "If she's able to do the work, she may stay."

Thus began my mother's affection for Miss Learn and learning. "How I loved the smell of new tablets and pencils, the wax on the newly cleaned floors and desks. Carpenter School was so special to me, I wished I had been a boy so I could have also cleaned the erasers for Miss Learn."

From her desk on a raised platform at the front of the room, Miss Learn taught all academic subjects to all students in all eight grades, which amounted to about twenty-five pupils a year. She approached her material with such reverence that it made my mother believe -- like her father before her -- that getting an education was important.

"Not only could no one take it away from you, it could take you places you had not yet dreamed. If our assignments were finished, it was possible to learn upper-grade material just by listening. Also, an older student could sit and help a younger student with lessons. With eight grades learning and reciting in turn, the power of concentration was not only tested, it was improved."

With awe, my mother remembers how Miss Learn also taught manners and character training, physical education and music, while also doing the work of a librarian, nurse, gardener, janitor, repairman, playground director and hot-lunch supervisor.

To this day, Mother is mystified by all of the expense and personnel involved with hot-lunch programs in public schools. Her teacher, she explains, simply had students bring leftovers from their evening meal to school in a Mason jar. She put these jars in the rack of a huge canning boiler on a kerosene stove at the back of the room. Promptly at eleven-fifteen each morning, she lit the stove. As noon approached, tantalizing fragrances of soup, spaghetti, roast beef and cocoa would waft through the classroom. Before lunch, students went to the basement, "where Miss Learn pumped water and watched each of us as we washed and dried our hands. During lunch she instructed us about table manners and the importance of morning ablutions. I loved that big word."

Miss Learn took time to enter students in contests with other school districts, giving them early lessons in self-esteem. "I was ecstatic to win a Parker Pen for the best essay on the sculpture *Black Hawk* by Lorado Taft," says my mother, sounding as happy today as she must have been on that day so many decades ago.

Though I never met Miss Learn, I have often sensed her

spirit looking over my shoulder. My children did, too, as they grew up. We have come to know her through the tales my mother told us. Like Miss Learn, my mother is a jewel. Beautiful and remarkable. A sweet disciplinarian.

Thank you, Miss Learn, for what you gave to her. Though all is vanished -- the school gone, you no longer alive -- still, you live on. I see you, forever young, standing in the doorway of Carpenter School. You are waving good-bye to your students as they mount their sleighs. Behind you is the large box festooned with pink and red crepe paper.

If it be true that the daughter is mother of the woman, then I, a woman, my mother's daughter, now tiptoe into your presence. You do not see me; you never will; but I slip a valentine into the box before I go: "To my mother's teacher, with love."

Beloved Books

When she was a girl, my mother couldn't wait for the library trunk to arrive at the one-room Wisconsin schoolhouse. When finally it did, she'd rummage breathlessly through its contents. Admiring some of the books, she'd rush past others until she found what she'd been seeking -- her favorite story.

Though today she can no longer remember its title or who wrote it, she's grateful to the Edgerton Library for having circulated it in a traveling trunk.

She and her sister had to work hard on the family's tobacco farm. Ashamed to be seen in their denim overalls, they'd hide whenever an unexpected visitor dropped by.

The book, however, offered escape.

"It was about three little girls in the loveliest long dresses -- pink and blue and white, with different colored sashes," my mother recently told me. "I'd look at the illustrations and imagine myself leading their heavenly life."

When I was in the second grade, I also fell in love with a

book. Each afternoon, I couldn't wait for recess to end and our teacher to read aloud a chapter from Gertrude Chandler Warner's *The Boxcar Children.*

The reading was meant to settle us down, but it stirred me up. I wanted to go on the adventure with the four orphaned Alden siblings -- Henry, Jessie, Violet and Benny. They found shelter in an abandoned boxcar, made beds out of pine needles and searched through a dump for dishes.

Never mind the cracked cup here or chipped plate there, or that their refrigerator was a running brook or that they had to cook over an open fire. Their exciting life was my idea of heaven. Here were children, self-reliant, making their way in the world.

In May 1994, *The New York Times* published a list of children's best sellers. Among "series books," *The Boxcar Children* ranked second out of sixteen titles. It didn't surprise me that the 1942 story is still going strong. I read it to my own children -- and to two nieces. Years later, both of them wrote to say how much the book had stayed with them.

When the youngest niece was expecting her first baby and being given a shower, I knew what to send as a gift: *The Boxcar Children* -- and *Goodnight Moon*, a book published in 1947 that ranked second among "picture and story books" on the *Times*' list.

Years ago, at a shower given for me, I received lovely presents before the birth of my first child. Yet, only one gift -- from the librarian at the school where I taught -- was for the mind and heart.

I remember thinking, when I opened the package containing Margaret Wise Brown's *Goodnight Moon* and saw Clement Hurd's colorful cover for the first time, that the gift wasn't soft and cuddly like the other presents and that it would be forever before it could be used. Forever has come and gone.

Soon, my infant son, transfixed by pictures and words, nestled on my lap. Night after night, we repeated the rocking-chair ritual. *Goodnight Moon* led to many more books -- and bonding moments as cozy as a newborn's kimono, warmer than any blanket.

In sending the package off to my niece, I thought how books help shape our own stories: in large ways, such as choosing a career, perhaps -- and in subtle ways, too, such as the long-ago gift that not only influenced what I give today but also inspired my grown son to hang a poster of *Goodnight Moon* in his room.

Once, when I was seven, my mother made me and my two sisters dress up and stay inside, where a photographer took our pictures. I wanted to go outside and play "boxcar children." Ever the tomboy, I couldn't wait to get back into my jeans and out of a long white taffeta dress with a green velvet sash.

The other day, while searching through some old black-and-white photos, I came across the photographer's results: the three of us poised on the front stairs. Sonja's dress had been pink, Karen's blue and mine white. With . . .

Suddenly, something clicked. My mother had brought to life her favorite book.

Only after time does a pattern, like a plot, reveal itself.

Miss Petty

On a visit to a library at age four, my father surprised himself and his older sister by discovering he could read. My childhood library was housed in a former church, but no such miracle happened to me.

Deprived of my father's reading genes, I slowly mastered the printed word. Still, because of Miss Martha J. Petty, The Boys and Girls Library was the place I -- and countless other children -- wanted to be.

A giant in memory, Miss Petty was scarcely five feet tall. Given another body, she might have stood taller. But she was hunchbacked -- bent over and closer to our height than the other adults who ruled our world. More than her nearness, it was that spirit -- caught dancing in her eyes -- that pulled us toward her. It transformed her into something startlingly beautiful and taught us about human dignity.

The first time I followed my mother through the Gothic doors of The Boys and Girls Library, I shyly inched my way toward the front desk.

"Miss Petty," said my mother to the delicate, elflike woman. "I'd like you to meet our youngest."

This stranger, the head librarian, greeted us as if we were the best part of her day and I the most important visitor she'd ever met. She led us on a tour down the nave of the former church -- past circular tables holding books and stereoscopes, past walls of books brimming with pictures, past windows filtering shafts of dusty sunlight and up the chancel steps to where an altar once presided under the vaulted ceiling.

Discovering I liked dogs, she helped me select three illustrated books for my mother to read to me. In the months and years to come, she introduced me to many new friends -- *Flicka, Ricka and Dicka* and *Snip, Snap and Snur* and *The Boxcar Children*. Better than Nancy Drew herself, she solved the mystery of what I most wanted to read -- the orange-bound biographies -- *Childhoods of Famous Americans*.

"Now," she said back at her desk on that day in 1948, "if you sign your name here, you can have your very own library card." In the stress of the moment, I failed the test.

"That's all right," Miss Petty said and did it for me. I was indebted for life as she handed me the glorious card and checked out my first books ever with her red rubber stamp.

Growing up, my friends and I knew nothing of her master's degree in Library Science from Columbia University -- only that, St. Francislike, she fed us more than crumbs as we flocked about. She never scolded if we forgot our cards, never punished if we already had spent our pennies meant for fines. We merely filled out "I owe you's" and tried to remember the next time.

If she was our guide to the inner world of thought and idea, then story hour was like Communion, calling us through the seasons. In summer, with sandy toes, we raced for the library's cool enclave in the basement; in winter, with frozen faces, felt the thawing furnace as we stood waiting for Miss Petty. Though we'd poke and push, we parted like the Red Sea when she glided through our midst and opened the story-room door. Our bones told us she had the gift -- the ancient art of storytelling. Never condescending, always authentic, she took us into her confidence. On little benches we roamed the world, traveled back in time, smelled the smoke of Indian campfires, bowed low in castle halls and fought in the Crusades.

By finding out about others, we learned more about our-selves. There was no shoving at each session's end. Only a quiet hush as we left in hallowed light, liking ourselves and one another a little bit more.

It wasn't so much the chairs and tables just our size. Or the benches and water fountain. Or even the books. What I liked best about The Boys and Girls Library was Miss Petty, who made it come alive.

A newspaper account from 1966 reports that on February 27, at age sixty, she died at home -- alone.

Miss Petty, it's not my book that's overdue, but a deep-felt thank you.

Longfellow

Culture can be caught like chestnuts from the spreading tree. But a tree must give of the fruit before a legacy can take root -- and grow.

In memory, my father looms tall, like a tree. It seems like yesterday I sat at the kitchen table and made faces at myself in the toaster. The scent of oatmeal, cinnamon and my dad's aftershave often mingled with his rendition of a poem by Henry Wadsworth Longfellow: "Under a spreading chestnut tree / The village smithy stands; / The smith, a mighty man is he, / With large and sinewy hands."

At night, when tucking three daughters into bed, he told us of Longfellow's own three girls and quoted *The Children's Hour*: "From my study I see in the lamplight, / descending the broad hall stair / Grave Alice, and laughing Allegra, / and Edith with golden hair."

I grew up on huge helpings of poems -- Robert Louis Stevenson's *I Have a Little Shadow* and others from *A Child's Garden of Verses*, Alfred, Lord Tennyson's *Ulysses* and Oliver

Wendell Holmes' *The Last Leaf.*

My father never could fathom why our teachers didn't make us memorize poetry as his teachers had demanded of him. "A poem can go through life with you," he said. "It can be a sheltering friend, like a tree."

Running off to school, I gave thanks that my teachers ignored such antediluvian practices. Besides, why did I have to recite poetry when I had a dad who could?

The son of Norwegian immigrants, my father was born in 1907, a century after Longfellow's birth. Dad was proud of the United States. He wanted his children to learn its legacy. He drove out West and stood with us at the Continental Divide. He drove south and showed us Shiloh.

One spring, in the April of my life, he drove us east to Massachusetts. At Boston's Old North Church, he quoted *Paul Revere's Ride* by Longfellow. Though we'd heard it often, it came alive as we viewed the belfry: "One, if by land, and two, if by sea."

At Longfellow's house in Cambridge, Dad guided us up the path of 105 Brattle Street. He explained that Longfellow had been the most popular American poet of the 1800s. Yet, after his death, his reputation plunged among literary critics.

What impressed me most was learning that Longfellow's three daughters and two sons were reared in this house, and that George Washington had lived there for a year during the Revolutionary War.

Still in family hands, the home Longfellow called paradise welcomed our little family. We saw the hall stairs on which Alice, Allegra and Edith had playfully descended for "the children's hour"; the study where he wrote many of his famous works; the dining room where he entertained Ralph Waldo Emerson and Nathaniel Hawthorne.

One fall, in the September of my life, I found myself back

in Cambridge. On Brattle Street, I spotted Longfellow's home, now operated by the National Park Service as a national historic site. Walking up the same path as thirty-four years before, I sensed Longfellow admiring his beloved view of the Charles River. I imagined laughing Allegra, Alice and Edith "descending the broad hall stair."

The moment revealed my father's legacy, planted so long ago. As a child, I wished in vain for a pony and fancy birthday parties. On this day, I realized I was given something far greater -- gifts that would flower over time.

Why are we often cut down just when we think we understand? When I returned to Columbus, my teen-age daughter asked about the trip.

"The best of all," I said, "was seeing Longfellow's house!"

So far had I fallen in my parental task -- and the poet, in popularity -- that my daughter looked puzzled and finally asked, "Who the heck is Longfellow?"

Be Careful
What You Wish For

Two doors down from where I used to live, grass covers the imprint of what once was. There in the back yard -- when Korea instead of Bosnia broke Earth's heart, when elms still lived up and down the block -- I learned a lesson:

Be careful what you wish for. It may come true.

Like spring. Or the neighbor's playhouse. When I was seven, I wanted both.

"When will we move?" I asked my mother again and again.

"This spring," she promised.

Eventually, the move to our new house came true. And beneath a neighbor's flowering cherry tree, I discovered a playhouse. White with green shutters, it had real windows and a door that demanded a key. But I didn't have one.

My father had many keys, which jingled when he took them from his pocket.

"You're lucky," I sighed.

"Don't forget," he said. "Each key means a responsibility."

His words, locked away in some forgotten trunk, didn't come to mind when my new neighbor, like a fairy godmother, granted my wish.

"Here," she said, dangling the silver key in front of me. "Dr. Gabe and I want you to have the playhouse, now that the girls are grown up. It can be moved to your yard, if that's all right with your folks."

"I'm sorry," my father later told me through my tears. "It'll just invite trouble. Every boy in the block will be down here fighting over it and jumping on the roof."

So a deal was struck. Like a stray cat, I was allowed to wander into the Gabes' yard each morning to play in my house -- complete with blue linoleum, white walls, corner cupboards, a built-in table with benches, plus room enough for a couple of chairs and lots of make-believe.

Day after day, while Earth starched the hyacinth stems and pressed her lilac dresses, I swept and scrubbed, spring-cleaning and feathering my nest with trinkets from home -- a picture of my dog, Nippy; a doll and highchair; a china tea set.

A friend and I played there often until, one day, war cries broke out in the cherry tree, as boys I'd never seen dropped onto the roof, climbed through the windows, crashed through the door. In the aftermath, I found not only a broken window and the broken tea set but also a shattered peace.

After that, I avoided the place. Yet, one hot summer day, when Earth held her breath, when I figured that most boys would be under a sprinkler or at the beach, I revisited my small dwelling.

Opening the door was like opening the oven. Making my way past dead flies scattered on the sizzling floor, I threw open all three windows. In swarmed angry insects, so many that they darkened the room. I fled out the door, but not before I was stung -- again and again. After treating my wounds, my father surveyed the damage and dislodged a wasps' nest.

Still, what haunts me most was the time I locked the playhouse, forgetting to close its windows. That night it rained and rained. When I returned a few days later, I found all the linoleum squares curled up like the toes of a genie's slippers. I couldn't blame that on the boys. Not even on the wasps.

Regret has a long reach. Had spring never come, I still would have been living in my old neighborhood, happy as before. As for the playhouse, I handed back the key -- and responsibility -- when my attention rode off in the direction of horses.

One day, several years later, I saw a truck carrying the little house down our street. Like a police escort, excited children rode bicycles alongside their new and precious cargo. With relief and envy I watched it go.

But I think of it year after year. Especially each spring. For it was then -- when Earth aired her green carpets and hung out blue skies to dry after a wash -- that she and I first rubbed elbows cleaning house.

The Flicker

"Hear that?" my mother once remarked about a blue jay's cry. "Rain's on the way."

"How could a blur of blue feathers be a barometer?" I challenged her.

She wouldn't back down, despite the bright day.

"That's what I learned on the farm," she said. "When a blue jay sounds as if he's making an announcement, it means rain."

Half an hour later, a shower proved her point. And the bird's.

On currents of meaning, birds dart through our days. In church we learn that a dove symbolizes peace. In school, that the robin means spring. And once, in my back yard, a brown flicker proved my father fallible. That insight shook me more than learning the truth about Santa.

One morning at breakfast, Dad complained that for the past few days a woodpecker had awakened him at five. When I was eight, I didn't know there were different kinds of woodpeckers -- such as the flicker. I could picture only the red-feathered one in the cartoon.

"How cute," I said. "Like Woody the Woodpecker!"

"Cute, my eye," Dad said. "Just about the time I fall asleep, he tries drilling a hole in the downspout near my window."

Throughout his life, my father -- a surgeon -- was stalked by insomnia and a ringing telephone. The more he wanted sleep, the faster it flew away. "How can I expect to operate when that character gets me up before dawn?"

"I want to see Woody," I begged, hoping the animated star might be perched outside.

"You're out of luck," said Dad. "He shows up only when I'm asleep."

Dad figured the bird was deranged. "Has to be, to go after metal."

The next day, while he made hospital rounds and I played in the yard, I saw a brown, spotted heap fall from the birch tree. Creeping closer, I discovered it was a bird -- breathing haltingly and with clotted blood near its broken wing.

Once my father had set my broken arm, and it had healed better than new. If anyone could save this bird, he could. Scooping it up, I carried it into the house and placed it in a cardboard box lined with soft cloth. I used an eyedropper to give it water, all the while wishing Dad were there.

When he finally arrived for supper, I first had him listen to the bird's heart with his stethoscope. And I asked a hundred questions.

"It's a flicker," he answered patiently. "It's called that because it constantly flicks its tail and wing feathers."

This one didn't. It grew more and more still.

Though my father was quiet, his gifted hands were busy -- gently fashioning a little splint from twigs for the wounded wing.

All evening I sat with the bird on our screened porch. "Quick. Come here," I'd call to Dad, again and again. Each time he crossed the threshold I'd point to the silent bird and ask, "Is it still alive?"

Early the next morning, I discovered that the flicker had become a cold stone. Racing upstairs, I woke my father. "Make it breathe," I begged.

But, though he was a doctor and though he was my father, even he couldn't do that. Later, when the sun left its nesting place and rose above the trees, we buried the bird.

Many months afterward I noticed a long cardboard box stuffed almost out of sight in the basement rafters. "What's that," I asked my mother.

"Oh, that? A Red Ryder BB gun. Your dad bought it to scare away some bird that kept waking him up."

In one exploding moment, I saw the man who was my father as if for the first time.

He wasn't perfect, just human, with weaknesses like anyone else. Everybody, I learned, makes mistakes.

Ann

In and out, back and forth along the strand of summer, we wove our way between two screen doors.

Had I known the year before that out of pain would come the joy of Ann and the best summer of my childhood, I might not have cried myself to sleep night after night. Instead, burying my face, I longed for my dad, who was far away at a tuberculosis sanitarium. When finally I heard the news he was coming home, I jumped every which way on the bed.

There was more news: Before resuming his medical practice in our Wisconsin town, he would study at the Lahey Clinic in Boston. His family would go with him, spending summer in nearby Cohasset while he commuted.

Ann, another nine-year-old, lived a few doors down from our rented Victorian home, which overlooked what the locals called "Little Harbor." In that magical seaside town, we were summer people -- more welcome than tourists, who couldn't find even a hotel or motel -- but certainly not townspeople.

My status made no difference to Ann, who accepted me unconditionally -- inviting me into her home; including me in her lemonade business; asking me to breakfast, lunch and the beach.

She was everything I wasn't -- tan, lithe and athletic, with brown eyes and brown hair fastened into a long, luxurious braid that fell to the small of her back.

Sometimes I saw her hair tumbling free, in wet tendrils, or framing her face and shoulders, brushed dry in the sun. I wanted long hair, braided or not, but I knew that I would have a long wait for my Buster Brown haircut to grow.

Like many other girls our age, we tried to dress alike, act alike.

"When my hair is the same length as yours, we'll be twins," I told her.

She looked at me doubtfully.

"Well, at least sisters," I said. And that seemed to satisfy us.

Days dove into weeks, weeks into a month. One day, leaning my head backward, lifting my shoulders, I felt my hair brush my back. "It's getting long like yours," I blurted into the phone. "It's growing, really growing."

At half an inch a month, though, it wasn't growing much -- not as fast as my friendship with Ann. I liked not only her but also myself when I was with her. Together, our two halves made a whole, someone new, a third person.

To this day, I love the sound of a screen door slamming, then the abrupt little encore before it claps shut -- for I'm reminded of Ann walking into the kitchen.

We were rich then, with the days spread before us, ready to spend. She and I would pick blueberries or ride bikes around the common -- past the white clapboard church and Town Hall -- or head to the library. In the heat of noon, with sandwiches and pop, we'd troop to the beach, spread our towels at the doorstep of the Atlantic and plunge in, emerging an eternity later. Dizzy from play, we'd flop on our stomachs and wait until the world stopped spinning. Sometimes, in the cloistered cool of late afternoon, we'd rest on an outcropping of gray, New England granite as Ann wove a spell with her flutelike recorder.

Three months -- and one-and-a-half inches later -- suitcases came out of closets.

"It's time to go home," Mother explained through my protests.

Why go, I wondered, when everything was right there -- my family and my best friend? Leaving meant I'd have to give up one. That summer I had everything -- my dad, my family, Ann, and enchanted Cohasset shining by the sea.

Early on the morning of departure, Ann appeared at the screen door. This time, she waited outside, her hands clasped behind her.

"Here," she said, handing me a soft and glistening coil, "now, we're alike."

Spinning around, she revealed that she'd grabbed a pair of scissors and chopped off her braid. If only I could have reattached the hank of hair and made her look like Ann again. If only I could have told her that her stunning sacrifice was the sweetest and saddest gift I'd known.

Pain and joy, joy and pain.

When I returned home, I faced more sleepless nights longing for a friend, a town, a summer I would not see again. Only now, having lived as long as I have, do I see how the two emotions take their turn -- in and out, back and forth -- in the braid of days.

Father's Letter

Long after my father returned from the tuberculosis sanitarium, I carried around a letter he had written. At night I'd remove it from my back jeans' pocket and leave it on the dresser. Every morning, like a daily devotion, I'd reread his blue-ink words, refold the once-white paper and return it to its traveling place.

Such is the power of a letter -- for, as John Donne said, it "mingles souls." Whenever I lingered over my father's words, urging eight-year-old me to be good and strong and help my mother, I sensed his closeness. The opening "Dear Lille Un" -- Norwegian for "little one" -- and the ending "I love you very much" expressed his feelings. But what spoke loudest of all was that he had taken the time to write. It said I mattered. I was worth the effort.

That letter and all the others to "Dear Marian and Children" helped bridge his absence. Back then -- before touch-tone and faxes, before computers and e-mail -- long-distance phone calls were considered a luxury. Even a decade later, during my college years, I wouldn't think of calling home more than once a week. Then, after only a few minutes, I'd hear Dad ask, "Whose nickel is this?" And we'd quickly hang up.

Looking back, I think it was a good thing. Otherwise, I'd never have received those tangible links from family and friends -- or put pen to paper to describe my own life. Through the years, like a flurry of homing pigeons, my envelopes winged their way from camp and college, work and early marriage. Preserved, a collection of letters can form a library of fleeting thoughts and passing days.

Recently, my mother happened upon a note I wrote many years ago on a trip to New York City. Knowing that a letter, like fine wine, gains greater value in the press of years, she sent it to my son.

He called me as soon as he had read it, amazed to have shared my thoughts about his approaching birth, about my choice of names and my hopes for the baby's future. He sensed me -- and his first stirrings -- in a context of history when I described the "hippies" in Central Park, the Eugene McCarthy rally downtown, and the train -- rather than plane -- ride back home.

A phone call has its own reward, but the experience, like life, is ephemeral. How does a young girl fold it and put it in her pocket?

Or frame it? A friend's father did just that with her first letter home from camp. And from boarding school and college and Europe. "It got to the point," she said, "that whenever I wrote him from some new place, I took great care, knowing it would eventually end up on his office wall."

Protected behind glass, pressed in an album or stored in the attic, letters leave a legacy of what we once were, of what once was. Years after both writer and reader have left this world, correspondence that joined their souls remains. Like the letters between John and Abigail Adams, or between George Sand and Gustave Flaubert, or between Sylvia Plath and her mother, Aurelia Schober Plath.

Too often what I now mail are scribbles on yellow stick-em notes that I slap onto news clippings and send willy-nilly into the world. Today, "less than 6 percent of all first-class mail is personal," Alexandra Stoddard says in her book *Gift of a Letter*, "and half of all household-to-household mail is greeting cards."

Stoddard underscores what experience tells us -- that "the bulk of (our mail) is junk mail, bills and charity or political solicitations." The art of letter writing is dying.

In the same way that they might inquire about the buttonhook or vaudeville or smoke signals, I fear that someday my future grandchildren will ask, "Grandma, what's a letter?"

"It's something your great-grandfather first sent me," I'll say, sharing my story.

"And then a year after he returned from the sanitarium, we visited a cottage on a lake. One day, when I was fully dressed, with one foot on the pier and the other on the waiting rowboat, I ended up doing the splits and fell in the water. After my sisters fished me out, I pulled the letter out of my jeans -- only to watch carefully wrought words blur into blue, unreadable rivers."

Still, for a time, I carried the wreckage -- a small talisman of my father's love. And mine.

Millicent's Chocolate Cake

Once, during spring break, my daughter's boyfriend visited our family.

"He loves chocolate," she told me beforehand, "just like you."

I decided to bake Millicent's chocolate cake to welcome him. I hadn't made it in years, what with all the talk in our house about low-cholesterol this and low-fat that.

Like my mother before me and Millicent before her, I used to make the cake often. After searching, I found the old recipe in Mom's faded handwriting.

She had written it down for me when I was a bride, copying it from the one given to her by Millicent, a family friend. Mine was spattered with the evidence of former attempts to bake from scratch.

"You're making Millicent's chocolate cake?" my daughter asked on the day of the young man's arrival. "Amazing."

No, I thought, Millicent was amazing. Soon the cake's warm fragrance filled the house.

"It smells like Jeffery Lane," my daughter called from upstairs, referring to our old house in Toledo.

I agreed, but the smell also reminded me of my own childhood -- and a woman my daughter didn't know.

When I was a girl, I'd see Millicent at least once a week, because her mother, Mrs. Dunn, was my piano teacher. I liked Mrs. Dunn, but I didn't like taking piano. If I was lucky, the student's lesson before mine ran late, and I could tiptoe past the living room -- as upright as the piano -- into the relaxed kitchen to see Millicent. She made Mondays bearable.

"How are you? Tell me everything," she would say, making me feel important with her questions. She liked hearing news from the "outside world," as she called it. Yet, her kitchen felt like the center of things, the center of the universe, where I could bask in her presence.

Sitting on a stool under warm light, I'd watch her move about in her wheelchair -- pulling out baking tins, sifting the flour, kneading dough. She had everything down to a system, with everything stored in the lower cupboards so she could reach it without help.

Then middle-aged, Millicent had baked from her wheelchair since polio crippled her as a child. Only once did I hear her refer to that life-changing experience:

"Mother had asked me to run an errand, and I put up a fuss," she said. "The next day, when I woke up, I couldn't move my legs. Many times since, I've thought how happy I'd be to run that errand -- any errands at all."

Millicent's baking provided a small livelihood, a great celebrityhood. My friends and I loved it when our mothers ordered things from her. Our favorite was simply "Millicent's Chocolate Cake." Mary Allen and I split one, along with half a gallon of vanilla ice cream, to celebrate our eighth-grade graduation.

"Ask her for the recipe," I urged Mother, hoping she might work Millicent's magic in our own kitchen.

"Oh, no," she told me. "Her recipes are secret. If she gave them away, she wouldn't have any business."

But one day, when I was at college, Millicent called my mother to say that, because she could no longer bake, she wanted to share her recipes. What she gave was more than a legacy in cakes and delicacies, it was a lesson in determination -- taking what life gives and making a life.

All this I remembered while baking her cake and frosting it.

"I'm off," my daughter said, leaving to pick up her boyfriend at the airport. When they returned, she introduced us. Then, looking to fill the awkward first moments, she led him toward the dining room, saying, "Come see Millicent's cake." Once again Millicent was helping make others feel at ease, just as she had done for me so long ago in her kitchen.

A week later, my daughter called from school. "Dave really liked the cake," she said.

"Actually, it was a little dry. I think I let it bake too long."

"That's what I remember about Jeffery Lane," she said. "Every time you made the cake, you always said that something about it wasn't right."

How could it ever be perfect? Millicent's touch is the missing ingredient.

MILLICENT'S CHOCOLATE CAKE

Don't faint when you see the ingredients. This was created before all the heart-healthy talk:

Use three 8-inch or two 10-inch pans. Grease bottom, not sides. Dust with flour.

Preheat oven to 350 degrees.

Ingredients:

2 cups sugar, minus 2 tablespoons
2/3 cup Crisco
3 eggs
2 cups regular flour or 2 1/4 cups cake flour
1 tsp. vanilla
1 tsp. baking soda
1/2 tsp. baking powder
1 tsp. salt
1 1/3 cups buttermilk
2 1/2 squares baking chocolate (melted)

Sift all dry ingredients into bowl. Drop in shortening and 1 cup buttermilk. Beat 2 minutes. Drop in 3 eggs unbeaten and 1/3 cup buttermilk. Beat 1 minute. Add melted chocolate and beat 1 more minute. Add 1 tsp. vanilla. Mix lightly. Bake at 350 degrees for 25 to 35 minutes, depending on your oven, and approximately 20 minutes for cupcakes.

MILLICENT'S CHOCOLATE FROSTING

1 package powdered sugar (16 oz.)
1/2 cup cocoa
1/2 cup milk, add slowly; when well blended add
1/4 lb. (1 stick) of butter or margarine. Don't melt. Beat hard.
1 tsp. vanilla. Mix well.

Cover sides, middle and top of cake with frosting.

First Corsage

Stopping inside a florist shop one Saturday last year, I was stunned to see a couple of hundred corsage boxes stacked inside the cooler. Tagged and tied with bows, they awaited pickup or delivery.

"Bexley's prom," said the clerk at Connell's Flowers.

Ah, sweet spring. Sweet adolescence.

But, I wonder: With today's prom talk -- "What limousine service are you using?" and "Where are you having dinner beforehand?" -- doesn't a corsage pale by comparison?

Back in my prehistoric teens, receiving a corsage was a big deal -- so big that I remember my first one. It arrived on the day of my first date. I can't recall anything about the dance that evening, and I remember little about the boy who took me. The corsage, however, looms large in my memory.

When the doorbell rang that long-ago afternoon, I was startled to open the door to a man holding a white box bearing my name.

"Kirsten Lokvam?"

"Yes," I answered nervously, accepting his package, "that's me."

As he left, I ripped open a small envelope and saw my date's name scrawled across the card.

Why would he send flowers? The dance was to be casual. My friends Ginny and Mary had helped me decide which sweater and skirt to wear; they weren't going, so I was to notice everything and tell them about it later.

"Maybe he just wants you to feel special," my mother said as I carried the box into the kitchen.

"I don't want to feel special," I said, moaning the teenage mantra. "I want to look like everyone else."

Opening the lid, I burst into tears -- overwhelmed not by beauty (the colors clashed) but by size. The corsage had to be the world's largest.

"I can't wear it. It's as big as a football," I protested. "I'll feel like an opera singer."

"Maybe it's a wrist corsage," Mother said hopefully as she removed it from the box. "It is.

"Here, try it on," she coaxed, slipping the elasticized band over my hand.

The moment she let go, the weight of the carnations, daisies, roses and mums spun the corsage around to face the floor.

"It's too heavy," I said, pulling it off and running upstairs to my room. "I won't wear it," I cried.

"You have to," she called after me. "Otherwise, you'll hurt his feelings."

If this was what dating was all about, who needed it?

"I'll try making it smaller," she said. "Don't worry."

Later, I crept down to the kitchen to take a peek. The counter at which she worked was strewn with flowers --

enough, I figured, to make a bridal bouquet and a couple for the attendants, with a few petals left for the flower girl.

After a while, Mother called to me: "Here it is, only smaller. And I made another corsage for your sweater. And these extra flowers are for your hair."

"Mom!" I protested.

"He wouldn't have bought them if he didn't want you to wear them."

There was no time to argue; he would arrive soon. I had to get ready.

When the doorbell rang, I glanced at my sad reflection in a full-length mirror. Festooned with flowers, I looked like a float in a Rose Bowl Parade.

Down in the front hall, my date stared up the stairs at me. His face registered disbelief, then disdain. With each descending step I took, he took a step backward.

"I'm sorry," I said, when I finally reached him -- in the center of the living room. "The corsage was really nice, but too big. We sort of rearranged it. But thank you; thanks a lot."

"For what?" he asked, edging away from me, retreating toward the window. "I didn't send you any corsage."

"What?" I gasped, wilting.

"If you didn't," I wondered aloud, pulling flowers from my hair and everywhere, "who did?"

Outside the window, a flash of two faces, a muffled squeal and the sound of running feet gave a reply -- Mary and Ginny, that's who.

Ah, bittersweet adolescence.

Beach Blankets

Corner touching corner, we joined our beach blankets on a bank overlooking Lake Michigan. Creating one huge magic carpet, we junior-high girls rode it almost daily under the summer sun. In time's hammock we swayed -- suspended between childhood and adulthood, between wide blue sky and gigantic brush strokes of bluer water. From our grassy perch, we viewed the beach below and our future on the far horizon.

These outings always demanded endless phone calls to determine what to wear and when to leave. Never going anywhere singly and rarely in pairs, we traipsed from house to house, collecting one another. By the time we reached Southport Park, our ranks had swelled to twelve.

While mothers ironed in cool basements, we stretched our baby-oiled bodies under the sun's heat. It was when Patti Page fell in love with *Old Cape Cod*. And Elvis tried to get us *All Shook Up*. But we resisted. Newly aware of our changing bodies, we stayed stitched to our beach blankets by invisible threads. To stand up in our bathing suits, to be vertical in a horizontal world, would invite unwelcome scrutiny. In such emergencies, we wrapped towels around ourselves for camouflage.

Anchored to self-consciousness, we rarely swam in the waves or jumped from the pier; no longer heard our shouts echo amidst the concrete pilings or searched for colored pieces of glass worn smooth by sand. As children, peering through these jewels on a sunny day, we had viewed the world transformed. Now we ourselves were transforming -- the rise and fall of our adolescent mood as unpredictable as the Great Lake at our feet.

But on this particular day -- when Grace Kelly had already married her prince, when we were beginning to dream of ours -- both we and the water were calm. Hard to imagine danger could swim beneath that shimmering surface. Harder yet to imagine we would ever leave the spot and grow up.

Instead, lying on our stomachs, we faced away from the lake and focused on the high-school boys throwing a football in front of us. Terry, the junior-high quarterback, was older than we and would begin high school in the fall. Newly accepted into a summer ritual, he joined the older swimsuited players who skillfully passed the ball.

Running back Alan "The Horse" Ameche, born almost a decade before Terry, once had tasted fame on the town's high-school team. Now, Dan Travanti (later to star in *Hill Street Blues*) was the current standout. Terry, everyone predicted, would become as great as the best of the city. Watching his agile body glisten in the sun, we saw why.

Later, he and the others raced one another down the slope. I watched them horse around on the pier. Clownlike, first one jumped into the water, then another. Terry's perfect body made a perfect dive. But he didn't come up. And he didn't come up. So I figured I'd missed him. Rolling over, I went back to sun-bathing.

Within minutes, a siren sounded closer and closer. Swerving onto the grass, an ambulance pulled alongside our patch of blankets. We jumped out of the way, forgetting our self-consciousness. Men leapt out carrying equipment and a stretcher. As they scrambled down the bank, a circle of kids parted, revealing Terry lying on the sand.

"He can't move," someone shouted. Silence fell as the men placed his limp body on the stretcher and hurried him up the hill. As they passed, I saw his face, pale and shivering. Seconds later, the ambulance sped off, its siren screaming.

Terry had struck the sandy lake floor. Paralyzed from the neck down, he regained the use of his arms but was forever bound to a wheelchair. That fall he sat on the sidelines at football games.

In a small way, we onlookers changed, too. We learned that life could be unpredictable, swallowing even the strongest. And we wondered how we could criticize our changing, imperfect bodies, when ours, at least, still worked.

We were growing up – each in her own way. Never again would beach blankets touch corner to corner. Together, but always a little apart, there were fewer and fewer each summer -- until, one year, they vanished forever.

Summer Crush

The catcher on a college team out East, Charlie caught my heart. He'd just completed his sophomore year, as had I -- only in high school.

That June, he blew into our Wisconsin town to serve as best man for his brother, who was marrying my sister.

The wedding set the stage for what, to me, was a summer romance. At the reception, Charlie asked me to dance to *Sweet Georgia Brown*. Afterward, back at the crowded house, we slipped outside out to walk along a moon-splashed Lake Michigan.

Yet, we shared nothing romantic, not even holding hands: He talked of becoming either a writer or a lawyer and of his first love, baseball. Still, his thoughts that evening took my breath away and made me feel like an adult, instead of his sister-in-law's kid sister. The best news was learning that Charlie, who hoped to play on our local semipro team, had found a job so he could stay through the summer.

Trying to snag him each day, I played a waiting game: I sat on the front stoop in the afternoon and strained to hear the sputter of his old '46 Pontiac. As he rounded the block toward his rented room at a neighbor's, I hoped he'd accept an offer for supper with my family. Or that he'd give me another driving lesson, so I could practice the "H" pattern of the stick shift and work the clutch and gas pedals. Or that he'd ask me to watch him play for the Kenosha Chiefs in that night's game.

Finally, I got up the nerve to throw a pitch, and I invited him to a summer dance. (My parents tolerated the age difference because, thanks to my sister's marriage, Charlie seemed like one of the family.)

My plan was to try to look like a college student myself. Raiding my older, but smaller, sister's closet, I uncovered a black sheath and a pair of spike heels -- which meant I'd have to lose five pounds and scrunch up my toes. I also bought all kinds of makeup, which I never wore, along with "powder puff pink" lipstick and nail polish.

"Would you like pancakes?" Mom asked on the Saturday morning of the dance.

"No, thanks," I said, waving them away. "I'm still on my diet."

That evening, faint from hunger, I put on five pounds of pancake makeup, eyeliner and mascara. Then, after squeezing into the dress and heels, I teetered downstairs.

Charlie barely said a word as I lurched out the door and down the sidewalk or when he helped me into the car.

Breaking our unaccustomed silence as we drove along, he asked, "What's the matter with your eyes?"

Later, as I hobbled about the dance floor, he noted, "I guess heels that high take getting used to."

Finally, as we sat out *Sweet Georgia Brown*, he said, in a simple yet distancing way, "That dress doesn't seem like you."

I had struck out without swinging.

Trembling from wounded pride, pinched toes and starvation, I washed tears, eyeliner and mascara down a restroom sink, wishing I could steal home.

I didn't see Charlie the next day, or his car drive by after work on Monday. So I was surprised when he turned up at the back door after supper.

"Want to go for a walk and get an ice cream cone?" he asked.

I was outside before he finished the sentence, dressed in sneakers, shorts and a summery blouse -- feeling like myself. Suddenly, I noticed a sultry-looking woman, with a certain "come-hither" gait, walking in our direction. I tensed, realizing that Charlie was about to suffer whiplash as she paraded past in tight dress and stiletto heels.

Then I remembered: He didn't like women who wore lots of makeup and dressed the way she did. We turned and watched her sway down the sidewalk, leaving a perfumed trail. Charlie gave a low, drawn-out, appreciative whistle before he asked, "Who's the cool chick?"

The game of catch was beyond me.

White Gloves

Ten pairs of gloves -- remnants of another era -- surround me.

In 1806, Napoleon owned many more -- two hundred and thirty-five cream-colored ones. He was said to be proud of his small, well-shaped hands.

Earlier, Queen Elizabeth I had been proud of hers.

"At every audience," wrote George du Maurier in his *Memoires*, "she pulled off her gloves more than a hundred times to display her hands, which, indeed, were very beautiful and white."

Growing up, I didn't notice my hands -- only that dressy clothes always meant I had to wear white cotton gloves, whatever the reason or season: church, a recital, a summer train ride with my parents. From the time I clasped my first Easter baskets until I held my wedding bouquet, gloves of various lengths and styles played a part in daily life.

Women of my generation knew about a white glove long before Michael Jackson did: We were always losing one -- and having to buy a new pair.

Centuries earlier, during Elizabeth's reign, the giving of gloves, especially perfumed ones, became so popular that universities presented them to people they wished to honor. (Elizabeth received an embroidered pair when she visited Oxford in 1566. During her era, people gave not only gloves as gifts but often "glove money" or "glove silver" with which to buy them.)

The ritual of wearing white gloves, like other customs, has nearly vanished today. Only a few decades ago, however, a pair was as essential to a woman's wardrobe as the necktie is to a man's.

Who can forget the pictures of Jacqueline Kennedy, in long white gloves, smiling at the inaugural ball; arriving at a reception at the Elysee Palace; chatting with Robert Frost?

Even though white gloves lingered several years longer -- and have not totally disappeared -- they seemed to fade from the scene after Jackie left the White House.

The Vietnam War, Woodstock, Watergate, even flower children challenged every assumption. "Proper" and "improper" switched places. With bras burning, is it any wonder that white gloves became passe?

At a summer wedding I recently attended, only one among the one hundred guests wore gloves. She stood out in the same way she would have four or five decades ago if she had not worn any.

A few days after the wedding, I unearthed my small cache and spread its contents on the bed. All ten pairs are made of white cotton. One pair, the kind we used to wear to proms and college formals, reaches above the elbow; some stop below.

Another pair, wrist-length, is trimmed with silver buckles. I remember wearing the gloves with a gray seersucker outfit on a plane trip in 1961.

Those with pearl closures I wore in 1966 on my wedding day. Was that the last time? Or the following year, when my sister married?

I keep telling myself to get rid of them, give them away to a costume department. Still, after all these years, I can't. Why am I saving them? Do I think they'll come back in style like old neckties? Do they remind me of my youth the way a '57 Chevy might remind a man of his?

I don't long for a return to the style. I could never keep cotton gloves as clean as my mother kept these. Nor would I ever be able to find them, as I'm never sure where I've left my glasses, umbrella, purse or keys.

When I come across the old gloves, however, I remember a flower girl navigating an aisle, or a tea table brimming with roses and blue delphiniums, or a band playing *Misty*.

The era was an expectant time of growing up, dating and falling in love; a time when the world waited outside the door. My friends and I couldn't wait to open it in our gloved hands. But first, after running downstairs, I'd always have to run back up for my forgotten pair.

Some night in the future, a retirement-home attendant is bound to find me sitting up in bed, trying on my outdated accessories.

Undoubtedly, she'll enter on her chart: "Additional displays of eccentricity."

First Frost

A first frost is the great divide. During some unsuspecting night, when the temperature dips below freezing for the first time since spring, frost-sensitive plants surrender.

Injury, chronic illness, the death of someone close also bring chilling change. The experience can form a person, either by withering the spirit or by steeling strength.

Survivors point the way.

Like the maple tree: Though its leaves die and eventually fall, they turn the color of a brilliant sunrise before their descent. The maple's scarlet crown is wrought only by this fearsome change.

Years ago, when my sister Sonja and I took our own greenness for granted, her life turned. One night, during her thirteenth summer, my father discovered her in a diabetic coma; she almost died. After days in the hospital, she recovered. She came back to life, though not to the one she'd known.

Sonja could no longer eat sweets. She weighed and measured all her food and gave herself insulin shots twice a day. Even now I can hear the needle and syringe rattling in the pan of boiling water on our kitchen stove, and I remember her leaving the room to give herself the shot. Why were we, her siblings, spared, while every day, twice a day, she endured the experience? We weren't half as strong. Instead, we pulled down the shade on a room called experience -- which she inhabited.

"In her despair, Sonja turned to art," my mother wrote. "When hopelessness set in, she created life."

Though in adolescence we think we'll live forever, it was then that my sister discovered existence is fragile. Pierced by the arrow of mortality, she lived more intensely, savoring each moment.

"With so much to do and experience, I wish I could have many lives," she wrote in her journal. "I never . . . felt so full, so alive. . . . It is a grand feeling hampered only by the thought that I don't have all the time I need to do all I want to do. I feel I'm approaching the finish line, racing to it, in first place."

Diabetes was the great divide, separating her from her former self, from her family and friends. Yet, through the ordeal, she put down empathetic shoots that grew into a greater understanding of everyone.

If Indian summer doesn't arrive until after the first frost, is human nature different? Like that warm and golden time, Sonja's inner light -- which earned her the nickname "Sunny" -- returned more radiant.

When she was a speech therapist, a girl, arguing with another pupil, fell down kicking and screaming.

"You're too nice to be down there on the floor," Sonja simply said. "Why don't you come back up here and sit with us?"

She co-authored a speech-therapy textbook, *Time To*

Modify. She spearheaded "The 'Affective' Education Committee" to help herself and other teachers better fulfill the students' emotional needs. And she was a student herself, taking ballet.

In 1972 she wrote in her journal: "My book will be published. My husband is pursuing his architectural studies, and we are happy together. I shall remember the feeling of intensity and being happy."

Once, when I complained to her that I didn't have time to pursue writing, she said, "No one has time. We make time for the people and things we love."

So great was her need to help others, she had begun the process of applying to medical school. She never took her first class.

In early January 1977, when temperatures dipped below zero, my sister, at thirty-six, died suddenly of a heart attack.

In spring, the elementary school where she had taught dedicated its auditorium in her honor. The town's ballet company attended and danced in her memory. And her pupils' words tugged at our hearts.

I take that to be a sign -- the way frost on the window tells me it's fall; the way a scarlet maple, like an emergency flare, sends up a signal before winter -- that Sonja had crossed the finish line, in first place.

Miss Bond

Like Dylan Thomas, "I can never remember whether it snowed for six days and six nights when I was twelve or whether it snowed for twelve days and twelve nights when I was six." But, whenever the first heavy snow of the season arrives, I am reminded of my brother, Chris, and the year he grew rich.

A storm blew in early that winter of 1959. A good omen for my little brother, who, at the age of nine, woke up that morning and decided to go into the snow removal business. Beating a path to the house of an elderly neighbor, he rang her doorbell. The porch light still glowed in the black, cold air.

"Why, Chris, what is it?" Miss Bond asked in a thin voice.

"May I shovel your walk and drive?"

"I don't take the car out anymore," she answered. "Just the sidewalk and the front path would be fine."

My brother tore through his very first job -- uneven lines here, spots of snow there. He wanted to reach as many customers as he could before the start of school.

Ringing her doorbell, he shifted from foot to foot. What should he charge? Fifty cents, seventy-five cents? He dared not ask for a dollar. Before he could speak, she handed him a five-dollar bill.

Bells rang inside his head. Astounded, Chris forgot about other jobs and hurried home for breakfast.

By first recess, everyone at Southport Elementary had heard the news. When it snowed thereafter, an army of shovelers trudged toward Miss Bond's. Chris always beat them to the scene. "It used to be the best feeling," he recalls, "to see the others show up late. They knew -- and I knew -- I had the big haul of the day."

Snow and five-dollar bills accumulated. Now and then, Chris took his growing stack of money down to the basement and ironed it, humming all the while like Moliere's Miser.

My parents were mortified when news of my brother's take eventually floated up to their ears. They called on Miss Bond, who opened her front door only a little and spoke to them through the crack. No, she would not take back most of the money. No, she would not let Chris shovel for free to make up the difference.

Yes, she reluctantly agreed, she would pay him less in the future.

The winter wore on; although Miss Bond did not open her door to many, she opened it, and her heart, to my brother. Like Pip to a modern-day Miss Havisham, Chris often sat sprawled on her living-room floor, reading books and playing with ancient childhood toys found deep within an antique chest.

Once, he was given a tour upstairs, where he saw an elaborate silver comb and brush and mirror atop her dresser. Miss Bond was the last in the line of a distinguished family who had been among the town's earliest settlers.

Alone and aging, she resembled one of "the few small aunts" described by Dylan Thomas as "poised and brittle . . . like faded cups and saucers." Dividend checks, strewn across tables, went uncashed. Bundles of newspapers crowded the rooms. And in the kitchen, half-empty bottles of cream littered the counters, along with a multiplying number of cats. During each visit, my brother stacked her mail, rinsed the bottles and emptied the trash. Out in the garage, cobwebs clung to her car.

"It was like she got to a certain point in time and froze," he says.

Miss Bond refused invitations to join us for dinner. Eventually my brother's persistence wore down her reclusive nature. During the first of many meals at our home, she appeared childlike and deferring. Later, she revealed a different side. When the men crowded around the television to watch football, she could talk formations and plays with the best of them. Chris beamed like a proud parent.

That winter, my brother amassed the staggering sum of one hundred and twelve dollars. When spring scooted into town, it melted not only his fortune-making opportunities but also his fortune: The first warm day, he hopped on his bicycle and headed to Dickleman's toy shop.

The money, he spent. The memories of a friend, who died long ago, he still has.

A child can learn a lot from shoveling snow: The early shovel gets the snow -- and the dough. Money should not always pile up like a snowbank. And, if an adult becomes frozen like the snow, it often takes a child to start the thaw.

Thanksgiving Train

Each Thanksgiving I see myself aboard a train, heading home from college.

Leaning my forehead against the window's cold pane, I watch Illinois fields rush to meet a Wisconsin prairie.

Forgotten pumpkins, round as a rising moon, color the gray ground, while the slate sky shakes loose a flurry of snowflakes.

A freshman, I feel light-years older than I did when I left for school; surely my parents will notice the difference.

As the train pulls into the depot, I spot them standing on the platform.

Or I remember earlier years, riding in the back seat of the car on the way to our grandparents' house in another city.

Are we there yet? How much longer?

As the car pulls into the drive, our cousins run out to meet us.

Or I recall my children's youth: When I pack boots, the weather turns springlike. When I forget, blizzards stall some cars and send others spinning into ditches.

Arriving close to midnight on the eve of Thanksgiving, we carry sleeping children into the welcoming house, where their grandparents are still up.

We take a journey each Thanksgiving, not only to where a table waits for us but also to Thanksgivings past. Retracing our steps, we travel an inner road -- discovering who we once were, reaching who we are.

When Mother was little, she would ride into town with her family to share Thanksgiving with Aunt Claudine.

She wanted to join the camaraderie at the festive table, but her aunt relegated the children to a table in another room.

As Mother retells the story each year, I can hear the disappointment in her voice. (No wonder, when she needed to set an extra table, she gave up her dining-room seat to one of her grandchildren.)

Once, when my mother-in-law was home from college, she helped her father pick watercress in a cold stream for the day's feast.

What was gathered more than six decades ago also lives on at our table.

This year, our daughter will miss our family Thanksgiving to visit her friend and his family in Boston. My father and father-in-law are forever absent -- and so is my sister.

As youngsters, she and I would color while sprawled on the living-room floor at our grandparents' house -- where even then, thanks to radio, football permeated the air almost as much as the aroma of roasting turkey.

We slept, the quilt of family covering us, on our way home. We didn't worry about fitting in; we just did -- always with a place at the table.

A few years later, when I tried squeezing back into my old highchair in the attic, I became aware of how much I had changed.

When I arrived home as a college freshman, I sensed another new self -- yet I easily slipped back into my old habits, allowing clothes to pile up on my bedroom chair, disappearing when dirty dishes towered from the sink.

Imperfection, however, isn't what we usually recall when past Thanksgivings roll down the track for an annual review. It's the perfection of faded memory -- like the image I have of my parents sending me back to college after Thanksgiving vacation.

Waiting on the platform, the three of us huddled close against the cold.

How I wished the train wouldn't arrive, just as I wished Sunday afternoon hadn't.

"If we never said goodbye, we couldn't say hello," said Mother, trying to cheer me.

"Christmas will be here before you know it," Dad said.

The train whistled and thundered near.

After I hugged my parents, Dad pressed a ten-dollar bill into my hand.

"Here's a little something," he said, "just in case."

Later, from the window, I watched my parents grow smaller as the train pulled me faster and faster into my future.

Christmas Tree Ship

When I think of Christmas trees, I imagine water, blue water; and three masts to which trees are lashed; and the scent of pine boughs above a creaking deck.

Each year, standing on the shore of Christmas, I remember the lake schooner the *Rouse Simmons*.

I never saw it, though. In 1912 -- thirty-one years before my birth -- it sank to Lake Michigan's icy depths, along with its captain, crew and eagerly awaited cargo: a shipment of Christmas trees.

As a youngster, I heard the tale, again and again. Scanning the horizon on winter days, when pounding waves painted the breakwater in ice, I had as much chance of spotting the ship as I did Santa Claus. Yet, it was part of the lore; the search, part of my ritual.

Not until 1991, and the publication of Phil Sander's *Kenosha Ramblings*, did I learn the specifics: The two-hundred-dred-ton, three-masted schooner, built in Milwaukee in 1868, was financed, in large part, by Rouse Simmons to help his Wisconsin town -- my hometown of Kenosha -- compete in lumber shipping.

By the early 1890s several boats on the Great Lakes had begun carrying Christmas trees from Michigan to Chicago on their last run of the season.

In 1910, Captain Herman Schuenemann acquired an interest in the *Rouse Simmons*, turning her into the Christmas Tree Ship.

"Chicago's Yuletide season began," Sander wrote, "when the Christmas Tree Ship arrived with evergreens lashed to her masts and rigging." The hold was full of "thousands of young pines and balsams from Northern Michigan. Residents would travel out of their way to see the ship in the Chicago River. . . . Her skipper would welcome throngs . . . aboard almost as soon as the ship's moorings were secure."

In 1911, Sander's father, a grocer, took his son "to the Clark Street bridge to see the schooner and to order trees to sell during the holidays. . . . My father greeted the Captain in German and we were given a tour of the upper deck and living quarters. Some 50,000 trees were stacked on the ship and dock."

Later, the captain invited Sander's family to return for a Christmas dinner of venison and bear roast: "The gathering was a joyful, old-fashioned get-together . . . I will always remember."

The next year, on November 22, the Christmas Tree Ship -- with its fragrant bounty and a crew of eight -- left Thompson harbor near Manistique, Michigan, for the three-hundred-mile voyage to Chicago:

"The sky was gray. The wind was rising, and the gale intensified. As the temperature dropped below freezing, a heavy snow swept the lake. The next day the storm . . . finally swamped the ice-coated vessel and it sank somewhere near Two Rivers Point.

"After the storm, a note from Schuenemann was found inside a corked bottle: 'Everybody good-by. I guess we are thru. Leaking bad. Endwald and Steve fell overboard. God help us.' "

Thirteen years later, the captain's wallet, "still intact with oilskin wrapping, and secured by a rubber band," was found on the beach near Two Rivers. For twenty-five years following the tragedy, after severe storms, fishermen in the area would complain of dragging up evergreen trees in their nets.

In 1971, when I was a mother of two, the wreck was discovered: "Still crowded in its hold and on deck were the remains of hundreds of Christmas trees. The divers brought up several trees, a china bowl, with letters R.S., and a hand-cranked foghorn" -- and later its anchor.

As a child, I, and others like me, had already raised the schooner. The phantom Christmas Tree Ship, Santalike, returned each year to my imagination, from a place far away, such as the North Pole. At night, during a winter storm, when the lighthouse sounded its foghorn, it sailed even closer, taking me with it, heading for open water.

Yet, each year, when we bought our tree, my family and I headed into town -- to a lot next to a filling station. Colored lights hung high above, like rigging; when the wind picked up, the looping strands bobbed and swayed.

"What do you think of this?" my father would ask, thumping a tree on the hard ground to shake out its branches. I'd see the captain striking a tree's trunk against the deck's planking.

Dizzy with the coming of Christmas, my wobbly sea legs could barely hold me.

Snowbound

When the world is snowbound, white magic can happen. One Friday afternoon during college, I scooped up my books and trudged through falling snow to the Northwestern Railroad station in Evanston, Illinois. I had decided on impulse -- without telling my parents -- to go home to Wisconsin for the weekend to study for midterm exams.

Soon, a train roared me north and met the night. An hour later, it dropped me off at the desolate depot -- which, to my surprise, resembled a way station above the Arctic Circle. No taxi could navigate the swirling ocean of white.

Hugging my coat closer and my books more tightly, I headed east through the shrouded town. I don't remember the cold so much as my repeated efforts to plunge through thigh-high drifts. The distance I was trying to walk is only about two miles. Then it seemed like two hundred. When I reached Lake Michigan and headed south, the blizzard tamed as wind subsided. Phantomlike, I passed my old school and hockey field, my friends' and neighbors' houses.

Finally, I spotted the bright beacon of my home and plowed up the drive. Reaching the back door, I lingered, like Hans Christian Andersen's Little Match Girl, to observe through frosty glass the scene within: There was my mother taking two loaves of bread from the oven and placing them next to a pie on the counter; there was my father, pipe in hand and laughing, entering stage right from the hall.

Thomas Wolfe, I thought, you can go home again. I knocked.

Suddenly I, the third of four children, knew what being an only child must be like. I was given a welcome like I had never known. Enveloped by my surprised parents and the simmering kitchen, I melted. After I exchanged dripping clothes for dry, we sat down to supper -- and the bread and apple pie. My parents hung on every word as I -- feeling heroic and without siblings there to steal the show -- told my tale.

Later, by the fire, Dad recalled John Greenleaf Whittier's *Snow-Bound: A Winter Idyl*, a poem I didn't know. Dad had had to memorize whole stanzas while in school.

I, the "snowblown traveler," listened as he recited: "The sun that brief December day / Rose cheerless over hills of gray."

He told of "A chill no coat, however stout, / Of home-spun stuff could quite shut out," and of the rosy fire in Whittier's New England farmhouse more than a century before: "We watched the first red blaze appear / Heard the sharp crackle, caught the gleam / On whitewashed wall and sagging beam."

Dad recounted stories shared by Whittier's father, mother, uncle and others who had gathered round the poem's bright hearth. Then Mother spoke of her memories.

Growing up on Wisconsin's Koshkonong Prairie, far from

neighbors and town, she had experienced blizzards, she said, "where you couldn't see from house to barn." Whittier had called his boyhood farmhouse "lonely"; she had found her childhood farm "lonesome."

"Very few cars went by the house in those days," she said, "and it was great fun if one would stall or get stuck in a snowdrift.

"Then we'd see the rest of the human race -- it was better than going to the zoo. I remember one elderly gentleman who had a mustache and walked with a cane. He was the oldest person I had ever seen. And he was smart the way he could play cards so well."

My mother, as a little girl, and the other children some-times had to give up their beds to the hapless travelers. Storytelling helped pass the hours before bedtime -- and could be fun, depending on the talent of those who were snowbound. Music, too, could charm the ear, if the two pianos, two violins and guitar were coaxed to life. When the adults played cards, she liked to watch, walking from chair to chair. Always, she said, her mother found food for the unexpected guests: "pies, cakes, cookies and, from the cellar, jars of meats and vegetables and fruits."

I, a traveler to my parents' door, was led to places I had never been. That night I fell asleep in front of the fire and only later found my way up to bed. On Sunday, we drove to the depot through plowed streets past scenes just like George Bellows' painting *Blue Snow: the Battery*.

I no longer remember what I went home to study -- only what I learned: We escape the narrow boundaries of our lives by entering other worlds. Even now, on a snow-bound night by the fire, when a log shifts, sending up sparks, I'll catch a "gleam / On whitewashed wall and sagging beam" -- and remember.

Lillehammer

Long before the world looked to Lillehammer, Norway -- host of the 1994 Olympic Winter Games -- people were leaving it for the New World. Before banners of five intersecting circles garlanded the town, two golden rings were exchanged.

I discovered them when I was a child. I'd often wondered what the highest drawer in my father's bureau held, so that day I pushed a chair over and stood on its seat, pulled open the drawer and peeked inside. Amid white handkerchiefs and pipe tobacco was a little wooden box. Lifting its lid, I saw two rings nestled inside: one with delicate pine cones etched across its surface; the other, plain, with engraving on the inside -- *Din Gunvor.*

I dared not ask my father what this meant, and confess my curiosity. Instead, over time, I pieced together this story:

My father's parents grew up just north of Lillehammer. The Lokvam farm was tucked high in the mountains amid

109

sturdy pines; the Thorstad farm was even higher -- not only in elevation but also in station.

Yet, both properties shared a breathtaking view of the Gudbrandsdal Valley -- a broad blanket of land that inspired Ibsen's *Peer Gynt*. Beneath the sweep of snow-capped peaks and far above a winding river, John Lokvam and Gunvor Thorstad fell in love. On January 8, 1898, the twenty-year-old groom and eighteen-year-old bride exchanged wedding vows and bands.

As the century turned, they gave birth to a dream called America. They and their little daughter, Gudrun, set sail for the future -- uprooting themselves from relatives and friends and Lillehammer. They homesteaded first in Minnesota, where fire burned their house and most of their belongings, then moved to Park Falls, Wisconsin. By 1913, both Gunvor and John had died within a year of each other, leaving four children -- including my father, the youngest, who was six.

After the second funeral, the children were taken in by an aunt in Eau Claire, Wisconsin. She was determined that they not be sent to an orphanage. Eventually, she was able to find homes for two of them and raised the other two -- including my father -- herself. No matter that Karen Lokvam Hanson -- John's older sister -- had two children of her own or that she was caring for an invalid nephew.

She had strength to spare -- the kind she had packed in her trunk years before, when she crossed the ocean to work for a "Yankee" family; the kind that had helped her, when she was just a child, leave her Lillehammer farm each summer to work as a *seterjente* -- a farm girl living alone in a high mountain cabin to tend the grazing milk goats and cows.

A quarter of a century later, my father, in gratitude, named his firstborn daughter Karen.

One day, fifty summers afterward, my sister Karen and I arrived in Lillehammer, fulfilling a vow to visit the land of our ancestors. The phone book gave us the name and number of a Kristian Lokvam living on the old Lokvam farm. Our cab driver, who also served as our translator, explained, however, that people in Norway sometimes take the farm's name as their own. Very likely, she said, this man was not a relative.

She was right.

Somehow, that didn't matter. We had seen what our ancestors had seen. We had driven past the ancient town's wood-and-timber houses, past the blue larkspur, past the glistening pines whose needles caught the sun.

It was like a dream, driving up the same country path our relatives had traveled down generations before, standing where they must have stood -- where Auntie Karen, when she was a young girl, must have scanned the valley and smelled the pine-scented air.

And it was good meeting Kristian Lokvam, who, though not family, invited us into the small farmhouse that held chests and tables and chairs from hundreds of years ago, furniture our ancestors had used, in rooms they had lived in and said goodbye to before transplanting themselves in America.

Though I never knew Auntie Karen or my grandparents John and Gunvor or scores of other Norwegian relatives, in the deepest sense, I do. Like concentric circles, we share the same center -- family. And family, like a sturdy conifer, can put down new roots in new soil and prevail.

Later, as the train sped us toward Oslo, my sister reached inside her purse and pulled out the golden wedding bands: one etched with pine cones; the other engraved *Din (Your) Gunvor.* She had carried them home to Norway in honor of our grandparents. As she slipped them into my outstretched hand, I knew that not only the rings had come full circle.

111

Trysil

Several summers ago, when my sister and I visited Lillehammer, Norway -- home of our father's parents -- I thought how easy our trip from the United States had been.

Just as it was easy for athletes and fans from around the world to travel to the '94 Winter Olympics in that country's leading resort.

Easy, that is, compared with what Norwegians -- and other immigrants -- endured when they flocked to America in the nineteenth and early twentieth century.

My mother's Norwegian great-grandparents -- Gustav and Ingeborg Gutru -- sailed to the United States in 1873 with eight children. Leaving behind their family farm near Kongsberg, they spent three months on a crowded ship before landing at Staten Island.

Dependent upon the kindness of strangers, they made their way in a new world and settled on a farm in Wisconsin.

How long did it take to wean themselves from the old

country? A granddaughter wrote of Ingeborg, who died in 1913: "She was always cheerful, (but) I had trouble talking to her, as she spoke only Norwegian."

My parents spoke only English as we children grew up. Somewhere along the line, in both families, the English language and the American way of life had been adopted. They had been assimilated.

Norwegian-American novelist Ole Edvart Rolvaag (1876-1931), who wrote *Giants in the Earth*, remembered the precise moment at which he felt like an American. He was twenty-four -- eight years after he'd left his home near the Arctic Circle, traveling first to South Dakota.

"I found myself on a streetcar somewhere in Brooklyn," he wrote. "A huge furniture van had got stuck in front of the car; the horses were balky and refused to move. (Our motorman) turned on the power, brought his car up behind the van, and began to shove. By George, those horses had to move! He shoved them for nearly two blocks, van and all, while the crowd cheered and the bell clanged. . . .

"I sat there in the car thrilled to the core of my being. Something had come over me like a wave . . . such a thing as that would never have been done by a European motorman, and I liked it, I liked it. Tears came to my eyes. This was America, my country. I had come home."

Something similar happened to me, only in reverse. When my sister and I reached Trysil near Nybergsund along the Swedish border, we were welcomed by my father's Norwegian cousin Solveig Saetre and her children and grandchildren. We stayed at their family home on a working farm -- one that had been commandeered by the Nazis during World War II.

We admired a hope chest, decorated with rosemaling, and other family heirlooms. And we feasted on a meal of elk that had been felled by our host -- my second cousin

Ola. After dinner, in the land of the midnight sun, Ola and his wife, Elisabeth, finished the haying. That night we fell asleep on feather beds, treated like royal guests.

While relatives may be expected to go out of their way, the kindness of strangers is unexpected.

At the end of our trip, after traversing the Sognefjord -- the country's longest fjord -- by steamer, my sister went one way, and I took a train to Oslo so I could return home the next morning.

For the first time I was all alone in Norway, unable even to speak the language of my ancestors. And I was hungry, but I had no food.

Seated next to me was a young woman of about eighteen who could no more speak English than I could speak Norwegian. We smiled at each other from time to time. I felt a little of what it must have been like to be in the immigrant shoes of my relatives.

Several hours into the journey, my seatmate opened a wicker basket and took out a sandwich, offering me half. Though I shook my head no, she insisted by holding it in front of me. She shared half of everything in that basket. I no longer felt like a visitor.

This was Norway, my country. I had come home.

Larger Lessons

I came of age in the 1960s; yet, it was my father, not I, who went to Vietnam. A stroke in 1986 left him unable to talk, but his life of action still speaks loudly. It's not so much a matter of what our parents say. The lives they choose to live offer the best lessons.

The legacy of fatherhood is hammered out of shared memory -- hugs, bedtime stories and being taught how to ride one's bike -- as well as matters beyond the child's ken. These experiences, some occurring before the child's birth, others outside the child's sight, help bring a father into focus.

My dad remembers his father patiently teaching him to tie his shoes. This is my dad's only memory of his father. It was to become a prophetic lesson in self-reliance. Dad's mother had recently died, and his father's death followed shortly after hers. In 1913, at age six, my dad, Leif Lokvam, was left to make his own way in the world.

Of the funeral in Park Falls, Wisconsin, he remembers

riding in the wagon next to his father's coffin as the horse-pulled cart made its way to church. Someone lifted him to peer into the casket at the funeral service. He saw two copper pennies, one on each of his father's eyelids, and wondered why. To keep them closed, he was told.

Perhaps it was these first encounters with death that led him, the youngest child of an immigrant Norwegian couple, to become a doctor.

After the funeral, Dad and his siblings were rescued from the fate of an orphanage by Auntie Karen, their father's sister. My father and his sister Gudrun grew up in Auntie's house. His other sister, Ester, and his brother, Jule, eventually went to live with other families. Jule, for instance, was raised by a distant relative in California. He and my father did not meet again for forty years.

Dad grew up in Eau Claire, Wisconsin, worked his way through college and medical school, and married my mother in 1935.

When he contracted tuberculosis in the fall of 1951, he chose a sanitarium far from family and friends. To keep his fingers nimble for surgery, he taught himself to knit. He gave us sweaters, mittens and mufflers that Christmas, and by Memorial Day he was back home in Kenosha, Wisconsin.

In 1967 my father, by then a past president of the Wisconsin State Medical Society, was still a busy general surgeon. He had three married daughters and a seventeen-year-old son.

One morning at the breakfast table he posed a "foolish" question to my mother. "What would you think if I said I want to go to Vietnam and help?"

This from a sixty-year-old man who had never been outside the United States.

My mother, who said, "If that's what you want to do, I

think you should," was braver than her children.

That October my dad traded the fiery glow of his Midwestern autumn for a burning landscape, the pounding waves of Lake Michigan for the incessant bombing in and around Can Tho. Far from his hometown, where the Elks Club and Symphony League clicked along, where golfers fought to get in one last round, where roses still bloomed to the left of his driveway, his new home was lined with sand-bags and barbed wire.

The hospital at Can Tho had five hundred beds. "But since it's often necessary to put two people in a bed," he wrote us, "the census runs up to 600 to 700 patients."

Dad was part of a special Air Force surgical team: three surgeons, four volunteer physicians, several nurses.

"Small hamlets and farms are mortared in the early morning . . . when people are sleeping. From morning until noon we receive many civilian casualties -- mostly women and children."

After surgery, he would visit as many as fifty patients in the surgical ward. "With open, draining wounds and incisions, the people lie on their thin pads patiently. . . . They are so contaminated that one can hardly bear to touch them, but you do."

Haunting scenes confronted him everywhere, from wounded and dying soldiers to the death of a young boy hit by "a booby trap, a white phosphorous bomb. It exploded, tearing off most of his hands, burning his body and face and eyes."

The eyes, my father told me later, glowed like copper -- bringing back the memory of his father's funeral.

Illness cut short his four-month tour of duty, and he was home before Christmas 1967. He was slender, stooped and sallow; we hardly recognized him.

His toxic reaction baffled specialists all the way to Saigon. The Surgeon General ordered him home.

Long before it became fashionable for his generation, Dad began to doubt the Vietnam War: He had seen it with his own eyes.

It was never Dad's style to lead a comfortable, tidy life. Besides his dedication to medicine, he was committed beyond the scope of his practice: helping combat tuberculosis through education fund drives, offering free medical exams to Boy Scouts arriving at summer camp, serving on countless community boards and supporting needy medical school students.

On Father's Day 1986 he suffered a stroke -- the summer before his grandson started college. Four years later his grandson graduated. But nothing in my son's education compares with the larger lessons we've learned from his grandfather.

Depression, often present with stroke patients, is absent in his case. He's too busy getting on with his life. He and Mother go out to eat. They've traveled by car, by plane, even by train -- once riding the rails all the way from Wisconsin to California.

Though his right side was paralyzed, he willed himself out of his wheelchair. He learned again how to walk. How to climb the stairs.

With a slow and shuffling gait, my dad rises to greet me when I arrive at the door for a visit. His arm in mine, he points out his roses to the left of the driveway and inspects his vegetable garden beside the garage.

Teetering downward, he struggles to remove a plump tomato. After an eternal moment, he succeeds. Smiling, he offers up the prize.

Silent, we communicate with our eyes.

Nine Months

The news came in mid-December: our son's early acceptance to the college of his choice. It was, he said, the best Christmas present ever. And so it was. Yet, it made me come face to face with something I'd been trying to avoid. "Nine months," I said to myself, "only nine months left until he leaves."

I remember news of a different sort and the words "nine months." How long that time once seemed, waiting for his birth. The days dragged on slowly, week after week, month after month.

There was much to do, however, to be ready for that moment:

A crib to be bought. A buggy, maybe even one that converts to a stroller. Perhaps a highchair, even though it will still be months before the child can sit in it. For sure, an infant seat. And a rocker, one to rock the baby to sleep in, to sing lullabies in, to read books in, with Baby on my lap.

Back then I did not think of tricycles or ten-speeds, summer camp or college. To me the future was my next doctor's appointment and Tuesday night's infant care class. In between those momentous occasions, time crawled.

If nine months then seemed an eternity, eighteen years would be infinity. So, when our son was born on July 28, 1968, we felt as if he'd be with us forever. Someday he'd go off to college, exiting the door of childhood. But somehow it was hard to believe. That day was always off in the future.

And so it is. But not for long. Though we celebrated with him over his college acceptance, I was secretly sad. Knowing how quickly the last seventeen and a half years had sped by, I knew September would come, and with lightning speed.

Like the pictures on a spinning top, the days are flashing by. Christmas has come and gone, New Year's, semester exams -- they all have melted into the month of March. With another turn of the toy, it will be June 11 and his high school graduation. The summer, which once stretched on, seemingly forever, will be only a bright blur as the months gain momentum.

So, on this rainy March day of 1986, it is not too early, I reason, to prepare for his departure, just as I once did for his arrival. With only six months left, I must ready myself for the letting go, just as I once did for the gathering in.

Back then I leaned on other women, already initiated in the mysteries of motherhood, to guide me through layettes and bassinets, formulas and feedings. Later on it was car pools and where to sew on the first Cub Scout Badge.

So, too, I now turn to mothers initiated in sending a son off to college. I partake of their supermarket wisdom. Over the artichokes in Aisle 1, a friend calls out, "He'll need a computer. Everyone has one. Whatever you do, don't make a mistake and buy him a typewriter."

The leap from crib to computer is a broad one, from Creative Playthings' crawlagator to '68 Mustang "awesome." Yet, through all these evolutions, we, as parents, are supposed to be resilient, flexible and unprotesting, actually cheering our children out of our lives and through the door. To have it otherwise, we comfort ourselves, would be unnatural. We have raised them for this moment, haven't we, to make their way in the world, to lead their independent lives?

No matter, the inevitable can still make us pause, and want to freeze time. Indeed, to turn back the clock. To those first nine months of waiting. Or to other days: the time we bought him his first pair of baby shoes, or when he had his first haircut, or the first morning of kindergarten. Or how about a regular, do-nothing day? What happened to spelling papers and shopping for tennis shoes, and ghost stories at night? When did he stop playing "Kick the Can"? When did he trade his last baseball card?

But, if I can't freeze time or bring it back, maybe I can slow it down. I'll try to listen better. Instead of worrying about the unmade bed or clothes in disarray, I'll explore the landscape of his mind. Instead of lecturing, I'll learn. About life and love, Earth and space.

And, should he seek any advice before he leaves home, I'll remind him of a time when he was three years old, his sister just a baby. To listen to her heartbeat, he put a stethoscope to her head. We have that moment frozen in a photograph. Over the years, it has made us smile. But, looking at it today, I realize suddenly the wisdom of his childish blunder. If we could all go through life feeling with our head, reasoning with our heart, the world might be a better place.

For years the crib, carefully selected so long ago, the highchair and other relics of infancy have been collecting dust in the attic.

Somewhere up there, too, are his baseball cards and beer can collection, his cowboy boots and hat. *Goodnight Moon, Pat the Bunny* and *Where the Wild Things Are* will be joined in June by his high-school textbooks.

Soon the bags will be packed. The trunk at the door. We'll drive off together, the four of us. Coming home, we'll be just three. But I must try to remember how every ending offers another beginning, the birth of something new. And without Goodbye, there is no Hello. I'm holding on to that.

Mother Emerita

On June 9, 1989, I quietly retired at the age of forty-six. Oh, yes, there were speeches. In fact, our daughter gave one of them. And a ceremony. But it had nothing to do with me, and rightly so. On that day our seventeen-year-old, the "baby" of the family, graduated from high school. When she accepted her diploma, I accepted a new title. I became a mother emerita.

I agree: A mother is always a mother. The love and concern for our children is constantly there, no matter how old they, and we, become. Yet, in a practical sense, active, hands-on mothering was over.

From now on, like England's Queen Mother, I'll be trotted out for family weddings and christenings. On Mother's Day and birthdays, I may receive, but hopefully not, the traditional corsage. Perhaps a card or two. Maybe a present. Then I'll be expected to fade gracefully into the background.

Retiring from motherhood is different from retiring from

music. No fans clamor for a comeback tour; there's no second chance to go for the gold. Peter, Paul and Mary, Diana Ross and Judy Collins may be one thing, but who wants to hear, let alone keep playing, a mother's old tapes of advice and cautionary lyrics?

Understand, the transition from mother to mother emerita is never easy. To go from being the center of your children's universe, career notwithstanding, to being expendable is a quantum leap. Or, rather, a plunge.

I remember coming into the nursery in the morning and seeing the smile of recognition on my baby's face. I was the sun, no doubt about it. I also remember the first time I accompanied my teen-ager to visit a college campus. Lumbering along, I could feel my reptilian tail scraping the sidewalk. No longer the center of her universe, I was extinct. Like a dinosaur having outlived its original purpose, I wanted to slink away to the nearest forest and disappear. But how did I get from there to here? From my daughter's babyhood to her young adulthood? For the most part silently and with unnoticed endings: the last time I lifted her out of the highchair and helped her into a youth chair; the last time I left the side of the crib down and she climbed into her big new bed; the last time I filled out a form for day camp and put away the roller skates and attended an elementary-school play.

One day the dolls were forgotten, the swing remained still, the ice cream man passed by unnoticed. Childhood books were moved to the attic, along with the doll house and Halloween costumes and once-prized stuffed animals. The white baby shoes, cowgirl boots, pink ballet slippers and first pair of heels all give testimony to the long stride from past to present.

Her brother left first. The wound slowly closed. So it will again. Yet, not before I think I hear her at the door coming in from track. Not before I wonder what she wants for supper. Not before the still stereo and phone make me long for the confusion that once reigned.

As each evening rolls in and rush-hour traffic speeds by, there comes a silence, an ache, I never knew before. A prelude, yes, when the two of them visited relatives or attended camp. Yet, then I always knew they would return -- to reclaim their rooms and grow awhile more in this space.

Now their visits are just that. Visits. No long-term settling in, they are like guests who stay awhile and then move on. Now their lives revolve in different spheres.

For two decades their activity generated mine. Rituals performed for them gave a rhythm to my days. My ear ever ready, from their first babblings as babies to their coming in late from dates, I now hear their voices long-distance.

But I also hear something else: a whisper deep within, reminding me that each ending brings the seed of a new beginning. If it is nourished and cultivated, strong shoots will blossom, stretching into the future.

As a retired mother, I will give birth to a new me. Adopt new patterns. My children evolved from infant to toddler to teen and now are young adults.

In the middle of my life, with angst and, yet, anticipation, I will try evolving in my adulthood -- by letting go of the parenting role and moving on.

The Doctor's Bag

When was the last time he closed his doctor's bag, reassured a patient with a parting word and drove the long way home? Did he realize after returning his black leather case to the closet that he would never again reach for it as he rushed out the door?

Probably not. Most last times slip away unnoticed -- like pulling off a pair of ice skates or reading a bedtime story. We fully expect to resume the activity, but we change, or our children change, and only later do we discover that another last time now rests in the pocket of endings.

Back in the '30s, and for years thereafter, he would grab the bag's leather handles and head into the night.

On October 23, 1933, my father delivered triplets in a rickety farmhouse in rural Wisconsin. As a child, I loved hearing how he had kept the newborns warm by nestling them in blankets and placing them on the lowered oven door -- the only source of heat.

Looking through an old record book, written in his hand

because he couldn't afford a secretary, I discover not only this delivery and others, but more -- everything from a man treated for a dog bite and anglers whose hooks caught them instead of fish to "Arthur S------: bullet wound, right foot."

In those days, when Dad made night house calls, my mother slept on the living room sofa to be near the telephone. Like today's answering service, she gave him the messages when he called home, and off he'd go on more calls.

The first night following their brief honeymoon, she remembered, "the phone rang, and I saw him dressing quickly. He explained there had been a serious accident at a bad curve on the highway. . . . He was gone in minutes. Well, I thought, I'd better get used to it."

He learned to say "Where does it hurt?" and "You'll feel better" in Italian and Polish and Hungarian to reassure immigrant families, and he resurrected his childhood Norwegian when he spoke with Scandinavian patients.

As a little girl in the 1940s I was more impressed with the searchlight he had installed on the car to find addresses in the dark, often after shoveling his way out of our driveway.

But nothing compared to the mystique of his black satchel -- a miniature laboratory and movable office. A fireman had his hat, a policeman his badge and a doctor his bag.

He kept it handy in the car's trunk. Yet, whenever one of my siblings or I was sick, he carried it into the house. Though still our father, he became something else: a doctor-father who, standing by the side of our bed, opened his bag and brought forth tongue-aahing sticks and ointments and syringes and the cold, silver stethoscope that shivered the skin.

In the 1950s, when he closed his general practice to specialize in surgery, he made fewer and fewer house calls. Long before his retirement in 1980, the bag moved to our front hall closet. Whenever I happened upon it, while hanging up my coat, I felt a certain sadness, the end of an era.

During the summer of 1992, on a visit home to my parents, I suggested to my eighty-five-year-old dad that we take a look at that long-ago friend. Though his stroke six years earlier had made walking difficult and speech impossible, he understood everything -- and nodded in agreement.

Carrying the black bag into the kitchen, I felt how the handles, brown with age, still carried the imprint of his grip. Before Dad opened it, his hands, in greeting, rubbed across and patted the leather. Then he unsnapped the lock, releasing the bag's familiar, medicinal scent. Examining its contents like a doctor examines his patient, he slowly scrutinized an old prescription pad here, a stethoscope there. I wondered what middle-of-the-night births or sickrooms or accidents rushed forward in his crowded memory.

When I sensed him growing tired, I said, "We'll look again another time," and put the bag away.

The next morning I had to leave. After loading the car, I returned to the back door and waved to Dad.

" 'Bye again," I called through the screen.

He smiled and gave a little wave. Seeing him at the table, so patient in life's hand, like a small and trusting child, made me go back inside. When I opened the door, he looked surprised, as if to say, "What's this?"

"I need one more hug," I said.

It was the last time.

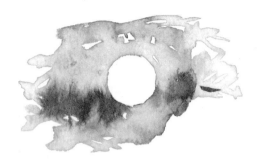

Same Moon

Magellanlike, the moon travels the round old earth. Though constant, it constantly changes -- from cradle crescent to round face to waning wedge.

Its disguises once puzzled my small children.

"More moon?" they'd ask, watching a wisp of one sail by on a wintry night.

"The same moon," I assured them, as if I knew.

Had I taken time to chart its course, I might have read the future. Instead, I thought the present would last forever. There always would be lunch boxes to fill, a swing to push, time for everything.

Yet, over and over, new moons rounded to full, and darkness went down to day. We sailed along. Each time my children embarked on a personal voyage -- a maiden bike trip around the block, the christening of a new school year -- they returned changed, older, new, like the same moon.

" 'Bye, Mom," a voice squeaked next to my bed. In the shadowy room my seven-year-old son stood before me, fully dressed, lunch box in hand, ready for his first day of second grade.

"But it's only three a.m.," I reasoned.

"I want to go early," he reasoned back.

"But your teacher and principal aren't even there yet."

"They're not?" he asked, dumbfounded.

"No. In fact, it's so early, the moon's still out." A peek at the full moon convinced him. He padded back to his room. Four hours later, I found him asleep -- still fully dressed, still clutching his lunch box -- on his already made bed.

Moonrise. Moonset. One full moon melts into another. Months plow the sky.

"Push me high, as high as the moon," my daughter urged, hugging a swing's rope when the yard was her universe. "Higher. Higher!"

Repeated attempts to launch her made the grass grow bare beneath our feet.

The moon rises. The moon sets. Months plunge into years.

The son who couldn't wait for four hours to pass is twenty-four. Under a mix of moonlight and city light, he and I climb onto the roof of his Boston apartment. I share a regret from forty years earlier: "I never got to see the Red Sox play."

The next day he takes me to Fenway Park. We sit along the third-base line near "the Green Monster." He treats me to popcorn, buys me a program. As he patiently shows me how to enter each play on my score card, I feel a tug, like a change in the tide.

I sense it again while visiting my twenty-one-year-old daughter in Germany. Once, long ago, I ushered her into a new world. Now she helps me find my footing in a foreign land. She breaks the language barrier. She shows me how to make change, use the phone, take the train.

Under a full moon in the medieval city of Schwabisch Hall, I watch her perform in an outdoor play. In the shadows, as she walks offstage, I catch a glimpse of the girl she once was, the woman she has become. I think of an empty swing -- and grass that grew back long ago.

The next morning, as I leave for Munich, she cautions, "Remember, Mom, be careful. Keep your things together. Do you have enough money? Be sure to call when you get there."

You say the moon has a far side that never shows? I have seen it: my grown children, my own middle age. In their waxing, my waning, experience has come full circle.

Margins of Motherhood

When my children were young, I once took a walk with my mother.

"Does it seem to you that we grew up quickly?"

"The time flew by, as if I'd walked through a revolving door," she said.

Because reaching that point had taken all my life, I thought she was exaggerating.

Now that my children's childhoods have become two felled trees -- I can count the rings and measure the length and breadth -- I realize what she said is true.

Motherhood -- the active, hands-on time in life -- has its margins just like childhood: When we outgrow the roles of mothers and kids, we evolve toward new ones.

Looking back, I see so much as a blur -- with the motherhood door turning faster and faster. What was the hurry? Why did so many of us rush? There was always the striving, staying up late, rising early, getting in another load of wash, painting a bedroom, dashing to the store.

Where were we headed? What were we seeking that made us always try to do two things at once -- talking on the telephone and ironing, folding clothes and watching television?

Even when the day was done, the last child tucked in bed, we had tomorrow -- the forgotten supplies to gather for a school project or baby shoes to be polished and left to dry overnight.

Even alone, we found ourselves cleaning the oven or rearranging the linen closet or shaking sand out of swimsuits. We forgot to praise ourselves in those private moments -- forgot that we worked and volunteered; forgot that we took on more and more, falling further and further behind.

Instead, we blamed ourselves for not achieving perfection. If only we had more time, we said, we could try being better mothers, making better meals, homes, yards, schools and communities.

"More" was what pushed us to race through our allotted days. We wanted to give our children even more -- lessons, clothes and things; and, in trying to give more, we often gave less of ourselves -- less patience and humor.

Comparing ourselves with our mothers, we often came up short. If only we'd explored further, recalling what we had so desperately wanted from them, and giving that, in turn, to our children: If we had remembered the sound of the door closing behind our mothers, would we have had so many sitters? If we had pictured again our mothers' hands turning the pages of a book, wouldn't we have read more stories?

Eventually, as one child leaves and then another, the revolving door slows down and finally stops. The mantle of motherhood, which we assumed would always adorn us, begins to disappear like a river from its banks. We go from being indispensable to dispensable.

Children, turning into teen-agers, help our transition by teaching us to let go.

"They slip you slugs all the time," a friend agonized. "You feel the heaviness of an insult. It lands in your lap, or you swallow it before you know it. They have to break away like that. . . . Yet, as a mother, you want to break away with love."

If we viewed our children more through the eyes of an accepting grandparent, would we find less to judge and criticize? Less to change and rearrange? Would we relax, delighting in them more?

Making their way upstream, offspring face their own moments of letting go -- graduation, college, work and marriage. Suddenly our sons and daughters disappear from our side. Alone in the doorway, we realize there was no reason to rush; it merely brought us to this moment all the sooner.

We begin to grasp the bravery of our mothers through the years, standing on the riverbank, watching us sail by. Can they help us understand our newest yearning? Is it still the same "Life's longing for itself"?

Yes, they say, as we reach shore and begin climbing the bank. They remember the feeling, which grew in them, too, before the doorway stood empty.

Hurry, they urge. Join us for a better view. A new generation is coming.

Mrs. VanDyke

One spring evening, Mrs. VanDyke set the table, fixed supper and went in search of her two young sons.

"Have you seen Don and Jerry?" she asked the children playing up and down the block.

They hadn't. In fact, they didn't even know the boys.

"Of course you do," she insisted. "We've lived here for years. When you see them, tell them to hurry home. Supper's ready."

Night after night she scanned the horizon, as if looking for a lost ship. "The last time I saw them," she said in anguish, "they were walking hand in hand over the hill." Yet, night after night the young sons never came in sight. Grown up -- with grown-up children of their own -- they sailed a faraway sea.

The woman, the mother of a friend of mine, was anchored in the past by Alzheimer's. A few years later, it claimed her life.

I see vestiges of myself and others in her behavior. What

mother of adult children doesn't ache to set the table as it once was? What mother doesn't hear the twilight shouts of neighborhood children and remember her own son and daughter playing "Kick the Can" and "Ghosts in the Graveyard"? Who among us doesn't instinctively turn in the crowd when we hear a child crying, "Mom," even though our youngest grew up long ago?

Parents make a lasting impression on children. Children, in turn, leave their indelible imprint on us. We are forever changed.

Though my son graduated from college several years ago and has lived in three apartments since, I still keep his room exactly as it was -- as though he were coming back home to live. I know better, but my behavior is like that of Mrs. VanDyke searching for her boys.

To navigate the straits of motherhood, we must chart a voyage between the gathering in and the letting go. At the beginning of our journey, we collect children and provisions -- from layette to bassinet, from play clothes to school supplies. Under full sail, we must remember to gradually release our hold -- from the first day of kindergarten to the first time at camp.

Surprisingly, our children age right along with us. They soon disembark for college and work and life on their own. What we thought was forever is finite.

Yet, the waters of memory are infinite -- and deep. They help keep us afloat as the children leave, as we sail on toward a brave new world.

Is that why my mother, a widow after fifty-seven years of marriage, writes to tell me that she is getting "our" bird feeder fixed, "our" lawn mower repaired? I, the third of four children, left home more than three decades ago.

Suddenly, I realize that she, like me -- like the mother searching at twilight for her once-young sons -- is trying to keep the home fires burning. As if someday, like a phantom ship, we all shall magically reappear.

I imagine my mother at the breakfast table. After a lifetime of gathering in and letting go, she is the only one left at my childhood home. I see her at work in the garden. There a rose bush thrives. Nearly half a century before, she transplanted it from our former house, tending it all these years. It speaks of the safe mooring she made for all of us.

Today she keeps busy and active. Yet, in her heart, like a sea captain's wife pacing a widow's walk, she watches and waits. Most of all, she remembers.

Jane Savage

In the spring of 1959, I didn't feel like singing. In the rain or elsewhere. Vonne Fenske had stopped calling. We weren't exactly "going together," but we'd been dating ever since he and his long-time steady, Janie Savage, broke up.

They had been a perfect couple. She was a cheerleader -- pretty, popular and friendly. He was his school's class president and captain of the basketball team. I remember his blond crew cut but not the position he played. I should, from all the articles about him that I pasted in a scrapbook as a surprise for him.

By the time the scrapbook was finished, so were we: Vonne and Janie were back together.

Knowing how hard I had worked on the album, my father, a doctor, carted it off to the hospital to give to Vonne's mother, a nurse. I was mortified. Mortified. That evening -- the parental "gun" to his head -- Vonne called to say thanks.

It was the last I ever heard from him. Or knew about

Janie Savage.

A couple of years ago -- shortly after Dad died and Mother's world became barren -- a woman named Jane Riley invited my mother to serve on the church's mutual ministry committee.

"Who is she?" I asked Mother over the phone.

"A Savage," she said. "There were three daughters, I believe. Jane's whole family started coming to our church when one of the girls married a Lutheran."

The Janie Savage? Suddenly, the high-school senior back in my hometown in Wisconsin was a grandmother. She and her husband -- performing a little mutual ministry of their own -- drive Mother to each meeting, calling beforehand to remind her of the date. One recent Sunday, when her husband was out of town, Jane took my mother and another widow to breakfast after church.

"Don't you think Marian has a lovely voice?" she said to the other woman. "She should be singing in the choir."

Though Mother protested, she was like a crocus beginning to peek above the snow. She went home, sat down at the piano and practiced singing hymns for more than two hours. When I called that afternoon, her voice had a vibrancy I hadn't heard in two years.

"I just might do it," she said, telling me about Mrs. Riley's suggestion. "When I sat with Dad, I wouldn't have wanted to be anyplace else. Now that I sit alone in church, it isn't the same."

For six years following my father's stroke, and many before that, she was always at his side.

Calling midweek, I found the line busy. "I was letting them know I'd be at choir rehearsal before church on Sunday," she said later, her voice sounding younger.

By Sunday, she was breathless.

"How did it go?" I wanted to know.

"I was so nervous and excited," she said, "that when I got there the door was still locked. I was the first one."

"Did you like it?" I asked.

"Oh, yes. I felt very much wanted."

Climbing back up to that choir loft must have felt like coming home. She grew up in one on the Wisconsin prairie in the East Koshkonong Lutheran Church -- from a babe in arms and a toddler on her mother's lap to a young woman singing at weddings and funerals. Her father, a farmer, directed the choir.

As a twenty-year-old bride in 1935, she joined her present church. There she sang in the choir until her children arrived. There she met her good friend Everetta McQuestion.

Today, after her long winter, my mother is the crocus emerged. Returning to where she began more than sixty years ago, she once again takes her place next to Everetta in the choir loft. Early Easter morning, you'll hear them there when music and lilies fill the air.

To Vonne's former girlfriend, I am grateful. After all these springs, Jane Savage Riley has given not only my mother a reason to sing.

Horseback Ride at Dawn

Even before we left on our ride, I was glad I had decided to go. Glad I hadn't fallen back to sleep after my sister Karen shook me awake. Glad I was sitting in the tack room, cradling a cup of coffee, watching her gather the gear.

We had slipped into our ancient childhood roles -- I, the younger sister tagging along; she, the older and wiser mentor.

"Why does this feel so real, more real than the world we just left?" I asked as I thought of her Wisconsin house on its still-dark street in town and of my life back in Columbus, Ohio.

"Because most things here have been made, not purchased," she said.

By "here" she meant her friend Louise's place, where Karen boards her horse. As Karen coaxed Freya and another horse from the pasture, she explained: "Louise put in all this fencing and built the barn and planted that huge catalpa by the corral when it was just a seedling."

Later, under the tree's white, orchidlike blossoms, my sister saddled and bridled our mounts. As she tightened their girths and gathered the reins, I felt my own constraints slip away: no longer a middle-aged homemaker and mother; instead, a younger sister growing even younger before dawn. Leaving the snug scene -- before the rooster crowed or barn cats stretched -- we rode deeper into the countryside.

Trotting through sweet, flowering timothy, through white yarrow and purple clover, through reddish-orange hawkweed and yellow St. Johnswort, we spotted a red-tailed hawk circling above. Here and there, we passed hundred-year-old homesteads where families who still bore the names of German and Norwegian immigrants slumbered on.

Like children, we cut through an unsuspecting farmer's cornfield, picking our way between the rows as tender shoots fluttered about our horses' hoofs. Looking back, I didn't see a single green flag trampled to the ground. We had won the unspoken game.

Finally, we reached a high ridge.

"Right here two nights ago," Karen said, pointing out the meadow below, "my friends and I saw zillions of fireflies. . . . It's called an 'aggregation display.' And when we rode through the shoulder-high grass, they glittered in the horses' manes and tails, and etched the tips of ears and hooves. It was as if Thor himself had struck an anvil with his mighty hammer, sending down showers of sparks."

That morning the waiting meadow parted like the sea, sending up sprays of dew, as Karen and I plunged into it.

As the sun galloped higher, we rode on, discovering pastures where herds no longer graze but where wild white roses have staked their claim. Up and down the hills, we retraced old cow paths.

As we passed a stand of birches, a great horned owl sailed by at shoulder level. Later, from a thicket, a fawn wobbled blinking into brightness; by a pond, a bird tried to lead us from her nest. "It's a New Guinea partridge," said my sister, who knows such things.

From the ridges we surveyed valleys and meadows. Encircled by countryside -- so far from highway and road, from town and steeple, from house and barn -- we were the only ones on Earth.

Suddenly we came upon two tents in a clearing. Carefully we rode by in silence, hoping not to awaken those inside. Yet, the spell was broken: We no longer felt unique. And the sun, like a summer hat, sat at a jaunty angle in the sky. It was time to return.

Riding back, I kept thinking what my sister had said about Louise's place: It feels real because things there are made, not purchased. The investment is of self and time, not money.

Isn't that true of experience, as well? Perhaps the most memorable times aren't the ones we buy, but the ones we make up or make happen -- like a ride at dawn.

Had I gone back to sleep, I would have missed the adventure.

I need more such moments, for I have been asleep too long. It's something I sense -- the way the throat can tell when it's thirsty, the way the heart knows when it hurts.

Too Still

When the house was asleep -- the phone no longer ring-ing, the dogs bedded down, the back door still -- sometimes I would slip downstairs and listen to the quiet, drink in the silence like a thirsty sailor.

Recently, a friend who has four children -- three of them younger than three -- brought that era to mind when she pulled up in a car with three child seats and the license plate "ITS MOM."

She, too, acknowledged sometimes staying awake at night just to absorb the stillness.

Twenty-eight years ago, as I fed my firstborn and heard the neighborhood children at play beneath the window, I couldn't imagine that my son would ever be old enough to play outside, let alone walk and talk and feed himself.

Before long, he left for kindergarten, riding off on his two-wheeler along with a first-grade friend. Walking behind at a respectable distance, I carried his little sister.

Three years later, she and her friend walked in front of me

and the friend's mother. Nearing Highland Elementary, my daughter suddenly gave a little wave, then pointed her new red shoes toward the schoolyard and ran ahead for her first day of kindergarten.

Moments earlier, she'd asked her playmate: "Lesli, did your mother say that it seemed just like yesterday that you were born?"

When the two no longer wanted their mothers trailing along, I'd watch out the family-room window until they rounded the corner.

Such rituals are at once unique and universal, like a bird instinctively knowing how to sing its call or how to build a nest. A young mother, I followed the eternal imprint of tucking in my son's shirt, brushing my daughter's hair, making daily inspections. My children stood framed in the doorway, lunch boxes in hand, as I saw them off with a kiss.

One year later, on September 6, 1977, I wrote in a journal: "Today, Tyler went off to fourth grade and Tia to first. . . . Today is a first for me, too. For the first time in nine years, I won't be planning or organizing or accounting for one or both of them between the hours of 9:00 and 3:30. There's a sense of freedom and a new beginning. There's also a sense of loss and the end of an era."

Year after boisterous year blurred into era after era of explosive change. My son is now the age I was when his sister was born. She is the age I was when he was born.

Instead of carrying home a worm in her raincoat pocket or rushing downstairs to tell me, "The moon looks like a giant's fingernail that got clipped off," my daughter answers a telephone at her summer job with "Housing Department." It catches me off guard.

One recent evening, shortly before her twenty-fifth birthday, I sorted through some boxes in the attic containing schoolwork I'd saved.

Although I had examined the papers when they first arrived through the back door, so often a pot needed to be stirred, a phone answered, an errand run.

That night, in the quiet house, I re-examined old spelling and math exercises, reread the comments from nurturing teachers. From my son's third grade year, I came across a sheet on which he'd listed his hobbies (fossils and stamps), his favorite sport (tennis) and what he didn't like (mashed potatoes).

I had forgotten that on weekends he liked "to bowl," and I wished, too late, that we'd gone more often.

Then I picked up a pink card bearing my daughter's first-grade handprint in white paint.

Inside the greeting I found a photograph of her, along with a mimeographed poem: "Every day you get discouraged / Because I am so small / And always have my fingerprints / On furniture and walls, / But everyday I'm growing / And soon I'll be so tall / That all my little hand prints / Will be beyond recall. / So here's a special hand print / For a special Mother's Day / To help you know exactly / How my fingers look today."

I placed my hand over the imprint of her vanished one. In that moment, I felt unique and universal, hearing the echoes of an empty nest.

Revel in the chaos. Drink in the noise. Soon it will be too still.

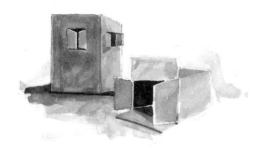

Moving

Home. Even when we're there, we hope to find it. Remember crawling under a card table covered with a sheet or playing beneath a painter's ladder? Best of all were the empty boxes. Joining them together, we designed larger dwellings to house our growing imaginations.

I keep trying to find my way back to that time -- when I could shape a space and feel safe and more at home in the world. Then one day, the boxes that had provided play on the back porch held the contents of where I'd lived my first seven years.

Since that wrenching move, I've resettled several times. In each instance, except for leaving home to attend college, my destination was dictated by outside forces. I've often wondered what it must feel like to be in charge of one's destiny -- to say, "I want to move here or there," -- and do it.

Had it been left to me, I would have lived in only one place as a child and another as an adult: no abandoning familiar soil every decade or so while I was still putting down roots.

Since 1935, my mother has called only two houses home, both in the same town. When I attended my father's funeral a few years ago, I sensed the vast safety net beneath her. The people I've known from childhood and the church in which I grew up offered her nourishment for body -- and soul. Such comforting security isn't achieved overnight. It's slowly seasoned, over a lifetime, with the give and take of days.

Those who say change is good for us are right. Yet, moving away prevents us from moving deeper into the same place.

For those of us who've had to move, though, the process is two-fold. There's the move -- and the moving on. Both can stress the spirit, because our homes contain the most tangible expressions of who we are. Yet, private refuge becomes a public place, as strangers evaluate our dwelling, deciding whether to buy.

Come moving day -- after years of trying, piece by piece, to complete the puzzle -- one's world is swept away like Dorothy's in *The Wizard of Oz*. Yet, we actually pay people to turn things upside down and move our "home" to a new location.

The movers transport us from here to there. We grieve, then sweep the past under a rug called "letting go."

Unceremoniously, a man hoists a chair out of the den. For him, it's just another wing chair. For us, it might be where a father once sat on his last-ever visit. The walls, the halls are hallowed now, witness to family history.

Long after I moved to Columbus in 1983, I struggled to move on. Not having a shared past, I found the first holiday season to be the hardest. At various parties where I was a guest, people with common bonds greeted one another -- they'd driven in the same car pools or gone to high school together. It made me miss all the more my Toledo friendships, nurtured over fifteen years.

Now my children live far from Columbus, and my husband's work requires him to spend more time in another city. When I'm the only one home, I have to rethink the definition.

"Are you going home now?" my mother asked on my last visit. I was standing in the house we had moved to when I was seven.

"Oh, Mom," I said, "I'm not sure where that is anymore."

"The whole world is your home," said the woman short on short-term memory but long on wisdom.

Her words reminded me of a visit last winter to southwestern Colorado's Mesa Verde National Park. Ravaged recently by fire, yet reopened after Labor Day, the park contains four thousand Indian ruins. At the end of the thirteenth century, following eight hundred years of carving out multilevel cliff dwellings in canyon walls, the Anasazi, or "ancient ones," moved away. Drought, perhaps, forced the tribe to merge with others.

At Spruce Tree House, a maze of one hundred and fourteen rooms and eight ceremonial chambers, a ranger pointed out a footprint on a ceiling, showing, he said, "that the ancients had a sense of humor." I recalled reading how young Abe Lincoln, lifting a younger child, had created footprints on a cabin ceiling. Cliff dwellers drew closer in time. So did the area's earliest settlers, from 550 A.D., when later I viewed primitive pit houses.

A hole in the ground. Shelter under a card table. Safety inside a cardboard box. High on a Colorado mesa, I felt at home in the world.

Goodbye House

With less than a month to occupy my home of thirteen years, I find myself walking about like a stage manager.

"Strike the set," I say.

My daughter introduced the notion:

"Mom, from the moment we moved in, you started setting the stage. Even though the curtain's about to come down, we have our memories forever."

She's right: We play our parts, then move on.

The stage manager in Thornton Wilder's *Our Town* says at the start of Act 2:

"Three years have gone by. The sun's come up over a thousand times. . . . Some babies that weren't even born before have begun talking regular sentences already, and a number of people who thought they were right young and spry have noticed that they can't bound up a flight of stairs like they use-ta."

Fifty-four seasons have turned round and round. The sun has come up more than four thousand times, as babies on the block have turned into teen-agers and our two children have become adults.

My right knee gives me pause as I bound up the stairs.

Emily, near the play's end, says, "Goodbye to clocks ticking -- and my butternut tree."

I bid goodbye to hemlocks holding snow, the silver maple standing watch in the front yard, the dogwood bringing the spring to the living-room window.

Won't I be lost without the little-leaf lilac in May?

How do I pack up the sound of a train as it passes in the night? Or the soft cooing that echoes down a chimney?

No longer will I hear the squirrels chattering high above or see cardinals taking a shortcut through the breezeway.

Left behind will be a row of flagstones that my daughter found hidden beneath the grass -- a new path as she started along the road of high school.

Also remaining will be the time capsule that my son buried in the back yard on the eve of his high-school graduation -- including a copy of *The Columbus Dispatch*, magazines, an unopened can of Coca-Cola, coins and paper currency, a family photograph and a letter.

Who will find it? When?

Who will remember where the giant pin oak reigned before a storm cut short its life?

I still see its phantom outline.

I also picture Rob Lucas' grandfather -- a former owner I never knew -- reading his evening newspaper in the living room.

"His chair was in that corner," his grandson recalled one day.

Each summer, roses -- wild remnants of the grandfather's cultivated garden -- carry me back to another era.

Who designed the house, I do not know, but I remain grateful for the way it collects the morning light.

Built in the 1920s, the structure will outlast my family and others.

Each, in turn, is its temporary custodian -- for houses own people, not the other way around.

I shall let go of ours long before it lets go of me.

On the driveway, a mosaic of hawthorn leaves tells me that time is running out.

"The dark comes suddenly now," a friend observes.

And so, farewell to the kitchen that saw less and less cooking but witnessed at least thirteen gingerbread houses. And to the back door, where friends left notes and parcels. And to the front door, where I won't be hanging a wreath.

Years and years ago, my son and I took a cue from *Goodnight Moon* -- his favorite story -- and started addressing inanimate objects.

Doing so made sense after we had repeated the comforting lines hundreds of times.

"Goodbye house," I say now. "Goodnight rooms."

"Tomorrow's going to be another day," the stage manager in *Our Town* assures the audience. "You get a good rest, too."

Martha's Vineyard

Here on Martha's Vineyard, as autumn, phoenixlike, rises out of summer's ashes, the smoke of memory pulls me back. Far from Ohio, even farther from my Wisconsin childhood, I have a sense of homecoming.

Fall can be a portal to the past. When changing winds turn cold, I turn inward. It's a time of battening down hatches, of sailing into harbor.

The seasons, revolving doors through which the years evolve, remind us that life is change -- the only constant. Heralded across this day's *Vineyard Gazette* are Henry Wadsworth Longfellow's words: "Nothing that is can pause or stay; The moon will wax, the moon will wane, The mist and cloud will turn to rain, The rain. to mist and cloud again."

I walk under my umbrella down Edgartown's South Water Street, past moored sailboats, past shingled cottages where the wind pushes vacant rockers. Though summer has slipped away, she -- like some gentle parent at bedtime

-- is leaving the door open just a crack: Her roses still bloom along picket fences, petunias peek from window boxes, and blue hydrangea bob beneath the rain. This is the beginning of the end of the year.

In front of the former home of Captain Thomas Milton, a seafaring man, is the pagoda tree he brought back from China in 1837. Then a seedling in a flowerpot, it looms over seventy feet and is said to be the largest of its kind on this continent. His house, built in 1840, now is part of the Harborside Inn.

Strange how standing in front of this white inn and facing the sea remind me of home and Lake Michigan; make me think of a welcoming fireplace and dilly bread from the oven, of afternoon light collected on carpets and bus money in a little bank on the kitchen windowsill.

As we become older, home isn't so much "the place where, when you have to go there, they have to take you in," as Robert Frost wrote, but a feeling we take with us and try to replicate for the rest of our lives -- a feeling of snugness, of being "safely gathered in."

We are imprinted with an eternal sense of "home" -- no matter how far we wander. Home can be found in a place, a person, a book, a melody. When we feel it, we know we're there. It is that safe haven where we find comfort. Where we feel anchored. It is a lifeline.

One of my earliest childhood memories is the nightly sound of my father softly padding through the house -- opening our bedroom windows for ventilation or closing them against a storm. Sometimes, before I'd slip back into sleep, I'd feel the grateful return of my kicked-off covers or notice him leaving the door open just a crack. Always, always, as our house creaked through the star-tossed nights, I'd hear the ritual of his rounds. The locking and bolting of the front and back doors, the turning off of the downstairs lights, his footfalls on the front stairs. As comforting as a clock's low sounding of the hours, he'd wind his way through our slumber, keeping us safe.

Even when I would return home as a middle-aged daughter, even after his stroke, I would hear him shuffle into my room to check the windows. Gone now, he would not be surprised to learn that just days after his funeral a gust of wind tugged at the unlocked storm door, breaking the glass.

On Martha's Vineyard, I try to imagine all the changes that have occurred since the once-powerful Wampanoag Indians inhabited this island. Their ghostly fires echo in the smoky mist.

Civilizations vanish. Parents die. Houses change hands. But a sense of homecoming remains. Like the north star, it steers us.

A Time To Gather

This is the time to gather, when broomlike trees sweep the sky, when fields, now empty, have filled our cupboards. This is the time to gather -- family and friends and food. Shut the door against the cold. Light a fire. Warm the soul. A time to reap, but a time to sow a harvest of new memories.

The eternal Thanksgiving table, like a long and bountiful bridge, joins generations to their past and future. Each year we return to it, even traveling great distances to be together.

Stopping the turntable of past Thanksgivings, I remember my father seated at the head of our family gatherings, the rest of us clustered about. I had advanced to the dining-room table in stages -- highchair, youth chair and finally a big-girl chair where I perched upon Dad's lofty volume of *Gray's Anatomy*. Seated next to him, I felt grateful when he helped me cut my meat.

Back then was when I learned to savor Thanksgiving --

the togetherness as much as the food. For, through the years, with the help of additional leaves, the table grew and groaned to accommodate a family of friends and relatives.

Once, an older sister and I scouted the breakwater by the lake, where she scooped up a miniature Plymouth Rock for the center of our table. At home she painted "1620" on it and plunked it alongside a brimming cornucopia to complete the centerpiece.

Minutes before the annual spread appeared, we could hear the hand-held potato masher hitting the side of a stainless steel bowl as Mother worked her magic. Like yapping dogs at our father's heels, we children watched him carve the roasted turkey in the kitchen. Now and then, he rewarded us with a shaving handed down on the tip of a carving fork.

At dinner, his rich baritone told the tale of a little tailor who "slew seven with one blow." His fist, for emphasis, always rattled the whole table. When laughter grew to rollicking tears, he fished for his handkerchief. Our camaraderie spilled over to more meals and a parade of leftovers.

When I was seven, my baby brother arrived. Soon he claimed a place at the table. Through the decades, the configuration continued to change. We children turned into adults, leaving home for college, marriage and work. Yet, year after year, by train or plane or car, we returned for the November ritual. Our babies joined the table and teethed on the same tall tales and family lore, as foil-covered chocolate turkeys patrolled Plymouth Rock.

Sometimes the day was shared long-distance. By phone, during my first year of marriage, Mother, like an air traffic controller, guided me step by step in making gravy.

Even after my sister Sonja's death in 1977, the day, in its deepest sense, remained the same -- a time to gather together, not so much to nourish the body but to refresh the spirit and our sense of family. Reunited, we remembered those no longer present -- and placed books under the youngest who joined the table.

Six years ago, after my father's stroke, Thanksgiving shifted from Wisconsin to Ohio. Sometimes Mother remembered to bring Plymouth Rock along with her pies and rolls and bread. Chocolate turkeys strolled the table for old time's sake. And, though Dad could no longer speak or tell the tale of the little tailor, he could still butter his bread with that familiar sweep, could still fish for a handkerchief.

Last year my grown son carved the turkey in the kitchen. I sat at the head of the table; my dad shifted to its shoulder. At dinner, I helped him cut his meat.

Last month my father died. Even though he and one of my sisters will be forever absent from our table, we are family, still one bridge, despite the distance of miles and years and death. When we gather together, that is the blessing for which we give thanks.

Turkey Duel

"It's you and me, turkey," I say early each Thanksgiving morning. Over coffee, bleary-eyed, I size up the bird, rereading the accompanying pamphlet as if assembling a toy for the first time. I vow again, fruitlessly, to roast a turkey at some other time during the year, so that by next November I can prepare one blindfolded. As family and guests sleep upstairs, I get ready to wrestle the latest slippery gobbler -- stuff it, truss it and tame it in a pan.

My shivering skin breaks out in prickly "turkey bumps" as I rinse the bird in cold water, then pat it dry with a paper towel. In a quiet house -- except for the newspaper's thump at the door, the coffeepot's occasional gurgle -- I lose myself in thought.

In a predawn, Thanksgiving kitchen, with night still draped about the windows, I feel especially close to my mother: So this is what she was up to all those years ago, before we descended on her for breakfast and a day of end-less eating.

Freshly showered, dressed in a sweater and wool skirt, she served tantalizing, homemade cinnamon rolls. Who would have guessed that only an hour or so earlier she'd had a tug of war with a turkey? The roasting aroma always announced the winner.

As I hurry about in baggy sweats, a package of Sara Lee cinnamon rolls defrosting on the counter, I recall how easy Mother made it all seem. So easy that I sailed on a sea of ignorance into my first year of marriage, docking three months later at my first Thanksgiving.

"Come for dinner," I said to a fellow-teacher and her husband. "Come for dinner," I said to close friends.

Fortunately, I stopped there.

I began making bread for the first time in my life shortly before I went to bed, setting my alarm twice so I could wake up to push down the rising dough. The bread turned out flatter, harder and more lethal than a brick.

My worst experience, though, was discovering that before roasting the turkey I'd failed to see and remove a bag containing the neck and assorted innards.

"What's this?" I asked, tugging and pulling it forth as I scooped out dressing for my guests.

I've known other turkeys, too. A "patriotic" one from the '80s leaps to mind.

For days one year, like every year, I debated how large a bird I should buy. My friend Ronnie heard I would be feeding fifteen people and suggested, without hesitation, a twenty-five-pounder.

She sounded so definite, so sure, that when the butcher asked, "How many pounds?" I, too, said without pause, "Twenty-five."

"That's awfully big," Mother remarked on the telephone before she and Dad arrived. "In fact, that's the same size as the Reagans'."

I felt a certain national pride. Still, each time I saw how much room the turkey took up in the refrigerator, then in the oven, but especially when I danced with it at dawn, I wondered.

The bird, however, proved to be a real trouper, making a memorable Thanksgiving dinner. A few days later, before my parents departed, I shaved the last of the meat from its skeletal remains to make them sandwiches. The turkey, Mother finally conceded, had been "the perfect size."

Yet, I'll never equal Mom at preparing a Thanksgiving meal. I still can't make gravy from the roaster's drippings in split seconds as the turkey "rests"; I still can't mash potatoes by hand only moments before we sit down to eat (I have to make them the day before and reheat them, so they never taste as good); and I still can't whip up Parker House rolls.

I used to sit at the table of someone who did, who made such dinners memorable. Struggling with a turkey each year helps me remember -- and give thanks.

From the moment I pull it from the store's freezer -- when it falls, stonelike, with a thunderous thud into the cart -- to the hour when it makes its dining-room debut, each bird gives promise of being my best one yet.

At least that's what I always tell it early Thanksgiving morning.

Advent

Time winds down to dark December -- a month of longer nights and shorter days, including the year's shortest. Thank goodness for the holiday season -- with its candlelight, fire-light and strands of Christmas-tree lights.

Yet, in the twinkling whirl of too much to do and too little time, I have to relearn the same lesson: When we take time, we make time -- by creating memories out of the minutes racing by.

Inside a mahogany box in the living room rests a miniature gingerbread boy, now retired. He is the only survivor of a couple of dozen ornaments that I helped our daughter make one Christmas long ago.

Rolling out homemade play dough, we cookie-cut rein-deer, Santas, Christmas trees, bells and gingerbread boys; then, if I remember correctly, we baked them. The next day, after pulling a thread through a hole near the top of each, we painted the ornaments. When they dried, we preserved them with a layer of varnish.

That year, Christmas didn't catch my daughter off guard: She gave part of herself when she gave away most of her homemade decorations as gifts. Some she kept for our tree.

Not even the varnish could preserve them, though, when they slipped out of eager hands or slid off a sloping branch, shattering on the floor. Now, only the solo gingerbread boy remains.

Like the ornament, another memory has endured: When our son was not yet five, his sister not yet two, we visited a farm to chop down our Christmas tree. So tall was the Douglas fir that its top had to be lopped off to make it fit beneath the living room ceiling. Using a small saw that his father had taken along, our son invested so much of himself in the task that he claimed ownership when the tip finally fell free: "A little tree for me, a little tree for me," he chanted, dancing about like Rumpelstiltskin.

Hoisting the prize onto his shoulder, he carried it all the way to the car. Later, in his bedroom, he strung a strand of blue lights around it and decorated it with paper chains.

"Do you think Santa will leave a present under my own tree," he asked, "so I can open it as soon as I wake up?"

"I think he might," I said -- and St. Nick did.

A few years later -- when our son was in third grade, his sister in kindergarten -- I helped at their school on the day before the start of Christmas vacation.

Her class party was in the morning, his in the afternoon. The day slipped away. As darkness fell, I piled the kids into the car to go on an errand before supper. I had heard of a woman who made floating candles, and I wanted to buy some -- for us and as gifts for others.

We found her shop on Main Street, down from the Post Office. As we opened the door, a little bell jingled to announce our arrival. On the counter, bowls of water held flickering candles.

The woman and I shared the usual "I can't believe how close Christmas is," and I blurted out that I hadn't gotten anything done that day -- because I'd been helping at the children's school.

Years from now, the woman said, what I hadn't done wouldn't matter -- only that I had been there. That, she said, is what makes Christmas Christmas.

Her words, like lighted candles, float down to this December. Errands that once seemed so important are long forgotten. Yet, I remember seeing the children's excitement at the start of their Christmas vacation and making ornaments with my daughter and chopping down a tree with the family.

Why didn't I take time for more such moments? There were other ornaments -- but always bought and never as beautiful as the simple ones made by a small girl's hands. There were other trees, but always precut and never as magical as the one that turned into two.

Each year I struggle to relearn the lesson of Advent: The season has more to do with preparation than presents. Christmas isn't something we can order through a catalog or hire someone else to handle. Each year we must create it anew, from scratch. In doing so, we illuminate far more than December's leaden days.

The Gingerbread House

Our first house was small, the shutters were lopsided, the front door was crooked and the roof about to cave in. Yet, to us it rivaled the Palace of Versailles.

Each December I shudder as picture-perfect, Martha Stewart gingerbread houses grace the covers of gourmet magazines. For nowhere do I glimpse the evidence of a child's hand. And it's the touch of a child's heart that turns the making of a gingerbread house into magic. Creating a masterpiece out of gingerbread may not be nearly as important as creating out of gingerbread a masterpiece of memories.

Every Christmas season my sister Sonja sent our children a gingerbread house from Marshall Field's in Chicago. So associated was she with the tradition that after her death my five-year-old daughter asked, "Who will send us our gingerbread house?"

"I will," my mother assured her. One dark night the next December the doorbell rang. There on the front porch was a package addressed to my children. "It's the gingerbread house, the gingerbread house," my daughter chimed cheerfully before the box was even open. Inside, there it was, just as she had predicted. But, like a broken heart, it had arrived in pieces.

"We'll fix it," my children declared, undaunted. They had greater faith than I. With a fresh mortar of frosting, we set to work, assembling a wall here, covering a crack there, improvising and making do. Resurrected and remodeled, the house was a strange sight, certain to be disowned by Marshall Field's. My children thought otherwise and proudly announced, "It's the best one we've ever had!"

Tucking away that memory, I vowed that the following year we would attempt to create our own. The next December we started from the ground up -- making the dough, letting it rest, rolling it out, cutting the desired shapes and baking the gingerbread. The aroma transformed the kitchen into a Tasha Tudor scene, even coaxing lacy snowflakes from the sky.

After lunch we assembled the house, decorating it with snowy frosting and a kaleidoscope of candles. A mailbox made of licorice, a reindeer cookie on the roof, a wisp of cotton for the chimney's smoke -- the children's imaginations took over.

And so they did each subsequent year, house after house. We would start at dawn and bake our way through the day, assembling roofs and chimneys, porches and railings. Each Christmas, as the children's hands and minds grew, the houses became more deft and durable, more elaborate and entertaining. From two-story to three; from mansion to castle; from barn to farm, complete with outbuildings.

Whole counters were used to display the ample structures, while powdered sugar provided a snow-covered landscape. Doll-house people were borrowed to make footprints in the snow, to skate on mirrored ponds and to toboggan down hilly slopes. Sometimes the houses were dated and signed. And always they were photographed with the proud architects standing alongside.

Then the inevitable happened. Our son and daughter became teen-agers. Their minds were elsewhere. Certainly not on gingerbread houses. If such a house was to be made, it would need a child's touch.

My friend's nine-year-old twin sons came to the rescue. As they labored in our kitchen, their double imaginations soaring, our son and daughter were coaxed into lending a hand here, an idea there. And a new pattern was added to memory's tapestry as the twins carted their gingerbread house home.

Last Christmas, five children from a neighbor's family came to assist. Once again our son and daughter, now adults, added a touch for old time's sake. But nothing they or I did could compare with the contributions from our five guests as they created their own special house.

A few days later, the twins' mother gave me a call. She told of a recent trip to City Center mall with her boys, now eighth-graders. On display in a store window was an elaborate gingerbread house, which easily could have made the cover of *Bon Appetit*. She'd been amused to hear one son compare it to the house he and his brother had made four years earlier. "Huh," he said, "not nearly as good as ours."

My children and I knew exactly what he meant. We'd learned that lesson long ago from a small house with lopsided shutters and a crooked front door.

HOW TO MAKE A GINGERBREAD HOUSE

Many years ago, a Swedish friend shared this ginger-bread recipe. As for assembling the house, Suzanne Karpus of Cornucopia helped to put the process into words.

SWEDISH GINGERBREAD
3 sticks (3/4 lb.) margarine
2 cups granulated sugar
1/2 cup firmly packed brown sugar
1 cup water
2 tablespoons ground ginger
1 tablespoon ground cinnamon
1 tablespoon ground cloves
1 tablespoon ground cardamom
1 tablespoon baking soda
6 1/2 cups flour
Cream the margarine and sugars until the mixture is soft. Add water, spices and baking soda. Mix in the flour thoroughly.

Divide the dough into halves and flatten into disks, then wrap in plastic wrap and refrigerate at least 24 hours.

ICING
2 egg whites
About 2 1/2 cups sifted confectioner's sugar
Place egg whites in mixer bowl. Beat on high speed for 30 seconds to break up the whites, then add sugar 1/2 cup at a time, with the mixer on low speed. When all sugar is incorporated, turn the mixer to high and beat for another 3 or 4 minutes. (You may need to add more than 2 1/2 cups sugar to get the right consistency.)

"GLUE"

(An adult-only job)

2 cups cane sugar, no substitute

Place sugar in a heavy frying pan over medium heat. After several minutes the sugar should start to melt. As it melts, it will turn from white to golden brown to darker brown. Do not stir the sugar (this will crystallize it), and, by all means, do not touch the mixture (this will cause a very bad burn). You should work with sugar while undistracted, even to the extreme of taking the phone off the hook.

If the sugar does crystallize, lower the heat and slowly allow the sugar to remelt. Be careful not to let the sugar burn. It should be a medium dark brown.

The moment to make the "Glue" is when you are ready to glue the walls together. It is necessary to work quickly. Once the sugar is off the stove it will harden tough as glass. It can be put back on the stove, however, and remelted.

TO FINISH RECIPE

When you roll out dough, use plenty of flour, but have a brush handy to brush off excess flour. Using a floured rolling pin, roll dough, one piece at a time, fairly thick, about 1/3 to 1/2 inch.

You might roll out the dough on a piece of cardboard, such as the kind the laundry uses for folding shirts, or the back of a pad of paper, or a manila folder. Then you can leave the dough on the cardboard and transfer it to a baking sheet by flipping it over. Be careful not to stretch or misshape the dough in the transferring process. A good quantity of flour under the dough will help ensure it does not stick to the cardboard.

Once the dough is rolled out, place the diagram of the house over it and cut out the pattern with a sharp knife.

Any excess dough can be cut into whatever comes to mind -- animals, windows, shutters, trees, wreaths, sleds, for example.

Place dough on a baking sheet coated with non-stick cooking spray. Bake in 400-degree oven until golden and firm, 10 to 20 minutes. Check after 10 minutes. The cookie should be set but not overly brown. It will harden as it cools.

The diagram of the house can be made out of a manila folder, cleaner's cardboard or the back of a pad of paper.

When the house is baked and cooled, "Glue" can be prepared. At this point it is great to have two pairs of hands so the walls can be glued and made to hold a 90-degree angle.

Dip the short end of a short wall and a long wall into the caramelized sugar, remove and hold them together. Then dip another long wall corner into the sugar and attach; dip the remaining short wall, and you will have done the four sides of the house. The liquid sugar can be drizzled in the corners to further seal the joints.

When the four walls are cooled, you can start on the roof, also with helping hands. Apply the sugar to tops of walls so the roof has something to hold it. Also put sugar at the roof point.

Decorate the house with any and every type of candy or cookie that appeals to you to make a sparkling, knockout gingerbread house. Use the icing as snow and frost and also to help cookies and candy stick.

The Nutcracker

Like the shining Christmas tree in *The Nutcracker*, growing taller and taller, my daughter -- suddenly grown -- captures my imagination.

She guides me as if she were Herr Drosselmeyer's carved Nutcracker and I were Claire, back two decades to the Kingdom of Sweets. The curtained years fly up as I see her in slippers or on toe -- one of two hundred dancers, twirling in turn, keeping time to Tchaikovsky.

She remembers my waiting at tryouts, car-pooling over icy streets, finding satin and lace for her first-scene dress. Best of all, she shares what can take years to hear -- her childhood:

"Whenever I see a pair of my old toe shoes, I think of Christmas and *The Nutcracker*. . . . Before I was in *The Nutcracker*, you took me to it, and I fell asleep waiting for Mother Ginger and her Gingersnaps.

"One day, when I was about five, a woman came into my ballet class. She had us all line up and go across the floor.

Then she began putting people against the barre. At first I was happy not to be pulled to the side. Then something . . . told me that I should try and get over there, so I did.

"Before I went on stage the first time, I remember standing near the big curtains. . . . When we stepped into the bright lights, the audience was reduced to shaded faces. We held the Chinese dragon over us and ran on tiptoe across the stage.

"A few years later, I was a mouse, then a first-scene dancer, then a frost fairy with twinkling lights in my tutu; finally, a tin soldier and a fan maiden. Frost fairy was my favorite, because it was the first time I was on toe.

"Tryouts, held in early fall, were in stages. First cuts decided, for instance, between 'non-mice' and 'possible, possible mice.' Then Mrs. Vogt would make another cut . . . and another. Finally, she'd announce the mice and the rest of the cast.

"I remember waiting . . . after class and seeing how light, reflecting from the street lights, looked on the snow. You notice light more in winter when the world is dark -- as in the darkened theater when the lighted Christmas tree grows.

"When I'd wait for a ride to take me to practice, there'd be *Rudolf* and all those great specials on TV. The next year, there'd be rehearsals on the same night. It was a fact of life.

"During the long *Nutcracker* performances, there was a lot of esprit backstage. You'd hang out with your group: All the mice, for instance, would hang together. Whenever any tutu dancer walked by, there was always a hush that fell over the pack of mice.

"I'll never forget waiting off stage and seeing the prima ballerina, who'd come in for the Dance of the Sugar Plum Fairy, and realizing that she was from a whole different league. I remember the muscles in her back. . . . She was from another planet, and she usually did have a foreign accent. I always thought our teacher was the best, the best of the best, because she was Queen of the Snowflakes -- until they flew in the pro.

"Every *Nutcracker* has its own fingerprint. . . . When I'd watch it on TV, it would seem completely different, a whole different nut, from the one we did -- like the way someone else's mother made peanut-butter-and-jelly sandwiches."

Before her reverie ends, I glimpse my daughter again in 1979, asleep in her jacket and mouse makeup, on a dressing room bench. When I revisit 1980, I see the two who take turns playing Claire signing her autograph book:

"Have fun in 'Nutty' this year," Melissa writes.

"You're a great first scene child. Keep dancing," Jackie urges.

Slipping the old ballet shoes back into a box after my daughter's visit, I study the smallest -- those worn under a dragon.

Today, twenty years later, my daughter still dances, still takes lessons.

Perhaps that's due to the magical gift of Herr Drosselmeyer -- or of Tchaikovsky.

Earthquake Tower

A toy made of cardboard and plastic is one of our family's most enduring heirlooms. I tiptoe around it in the attic, careful not to disturb its tentative tilt, for one brush of my skirt will send it toppling. It is, after all, an Earthquake Tower.

This story begins in 1976, the day before Christmas. It's morning. And I am in the midst of baking one more batch of Christmas cookies, while my eight-year-old son and five-year-old daughter play outside in the new snow.

The phone rings. It's my sister Sonja calling from Evanston. "What are you giving the children?" she asks.

"Tia's big present is a doll house," I tell her excitedly. "A carpenter made an exact replica of the front of our house."

"What about Tyler?"

"Well," I explain confidentially, "he wants this thing called Earthquake Tower. That's all he talks about, but we didn't get it. It's just a piece of junk -- cardboard and plastic. You wouldn't believe what they're asking for it. It's so stupid. I mean, it's meant to fall down. You barely touch it and it goes sprawling everywhere."

Silence on the other end of the phone. I expect her to agree with me. Instead she says, "So, it may not end up in your attic as a family heirloom like the doll house. It may last only a few days. But it will make Ty's Christmas."

"Sonja," I wail. She's making me feel uncomfortable. I reel off presents we've gotten him, ones we think will be good for him.

"Look at it this way," she says. "Obviously, you value the doll house. You probably wish you had gotten one when you were little. In a way, you're giving yourself the present you never got. Ty knows you couldn't care less about an Earthquake Tower. But, if you give it to him, it will show that you honor and respect his values, even if they're different from your own."

I can't hang up the phone fast enough. Running upstairs to find my husband, I say, "Quick, hurry. Sonja says we've got to get Ty the Earthquake Tower." He takes it all in, agrees -- and drives off in pursuit. I stay to watch the children and finish the baking and worry. It's December twenty-fourth. What if he can't find one?

Later, my husband tells me that he raced to the store and found the right aisle. Miraculously, there was one Earthquake Tower left.

Home movies from the next morning show our son bursting into the room and dropping to his knees before the assembled toy. With a shy blow, he knocks it down. Then he and his sister reassemble it, and down it goes all over again. The doll house is almost ignored. Our daughter checks it out. Our son admires it politely. Then they both go running back to the tumbling Earthquake Tower.

A few days later, toys still scattered beneath our tree, my sister died unexpectedly at the age of thirty-six. Ever

175

since, the flimsy Earthquake Tower has been a sturdy symbol of Christmas giving and what she taught us.

Years later, friends tell us their young son wants a little electric toy car for Christmas.

"Get it," my husband and I say in unison.

"But it's so expensive."

"Get it," we say. "You'll probably spend the same amount buying him toys he doesn't want. Make it his only present if you have to. Tell relatives who want to know what to get him to help chip in. But get it, if you possibly can." Then we share the story of the Earthquake Tower.

"But will he think he can always have whatever he wants? Will it make him materialistic?"

That didn't happen to our son, we explain.

Later they tell us they bought the toy car. On Christmas it will be waiting under the tree. We share their excitement.

In the attic to collect our Christmas ornaments, I give the venerable Earthquake Tower a knowing nod. I am transported back to that Christmas, when our children are young and my sister is alive. She is talking to me on the phone. I see our son's expression on Christmas morning. I watch him and our daughter play with the priceless toy.

If our house were on fire, and we were all safe outside, I think it would be the one thing I would rush back inside to save. But, even if something happened to it, I still would have the towering memory of that happy Christmas.

New Skates

Bills, not Christmas cards, collect in mailboxes. Abandoned Christmas trees litter curbs. January 6 marked the Twelfth Day of Christmas -- the end of the holiday season.

So let us raise a toast in praise of the everyday. Routine is a welcome relief. It gives us freedom -- time to fold the laundry, clean the garage or even break in a pair of new skates. Ordinary days play a supporting role to superstar holidays, which twirl center stage. Sometimes, though, an ordinary day steals the show.

All I wanted for Christmas 1953 was a pair of new skates. Each winter, Mr. and Mrs. Anderson -- an elderly couple whose mansion overlooked Lake Michigan -- had a groundskeeper transform their yard into a skater's paradise. Beneath an oak's branches, which held a floodlight, a wooden bench provided a place to lace up. There I'd sit -- when I wasn't wobbling about the ice on hand-me-down black hockey skates -- and watch Ginny and Joan sail by. If I only had white figure skates instead of boy's skates with socks stuffed in the toes, I could skate like my friends.

Christmas morning was a show-stopper. Under the tree I found a large square box. Ripping off ribbon and paper, I saw silver blades, serrated at the toe, sparkling up at me. Like the great Sonja Henie's, my figure skates were whiter than snow. Hugging them close and smelling the leather's brand-new scent, I wanted to rush outside and try them.

"Not now," my parents said. "Everyone is opening presents. And company is coming . . ."

One by one, the footlights went out. Down came the curtain. I bided my time.

The next morning, I bounded out of bed and headed to Andersons' rink with my friends. I -- the girl no one thought could skate -- would finally show them. Laced up and rushing onto the ice, I promptly fell down: I had forgotten to remove the rubber guards.

I fell many times thereafter, even without the guards. The blades' jagged tips kept tripping me up, and I began thinking more kindly of my old black hockey skates. Day after day I practiced, until eventually I could circle the pond like the other skaters.

Still, I couldn't do any solo, show-off stuff like "Shoot the Duck" -- where the skater bends at the knees, shifts her weight to her left side, picks up the tip of her right skate with her right hand and extends her leg straight as a rifle. Joan could do that -- and half a dozen other tricks. I tried consoling myself by remembering that she lived across the street from the rink and could skate whenever she wished, even before school.

I, who lived blocks away, had to content myself with skating after school. Every afternoon, I'd drop off my books at home and pick up my skates and rush off to the Andersons'. If only a few others were there, I'd practice

"Shoot the Duck." As soon as the ice filled up, I'd stop. Then I'd try to outlast the other skaters, watching them melt away to warm and waiting kitchens, and I'd practice again. I always imagined Mr. and Mrs. Anderson behind the windows, cheering me on or gasping when I fell.

Early one evening, when the moon over the lake hung lower than the tree's bright floodlight, I practiced on alone. Flying fast, I bent down, shifted my weight, picked up a skate and extended my leg. It didn't matter that no one was there, that perhaps not even the Andersons were watching from dark windows. I knew -- and that was enough. With wind rushing by my unscarfed ears, I felt confident that this time I would make it across the ice. And I did, stopped only by the snowbank.

I hurried home, the skates slung around my neck. Still, I glided -- giddy with the gift I had given myself. Time after time, I had been going in circles; yet, within the confines of repetition, I had advanced. I don't remember what day it was, but the feeling was better than Christmas.

Like turns on a rink, ordinary days come round and round. Their predictability lulls us into thinking that things remain the same. Celebratory days, however, highlight what has been happening all along: never-ending, circular change -- a wedding here, a christening there, a birthday reminding us that another year has vanished.

We need the ordinary days to make a holiday stand out; we need the holidays to make us appreciate an everyday. If I could relive a moment, it wouldn't be a noisy, special day, but a quiet, everyday one -- so quiet that I'd hear the ice make shavings as my skates came to a stop.

Lambie

The forgotten lamb sleeps on a cupboard shelf in the upstairs hallway. Yet, whenever "Lambie" is mentioned, he's remembered. Even a newspaper article can bring him to mind -- like the recent report that Jane Pauley had found a child's teddy bear inside a taxi. Pauley, a mother of three, tried locating its owner: She understands, she said, the panic that seizes a child when separated from a security toy.

These days, Lambie -- a floppy, stuffed animal -- is out of sight and thought. A quarter of a century ago, however, events turned on his whereabouts -- the time, for instance, he was accidentally left behind in a church nursery. Later, at home, our fifteen-month-old son realized that his favorite toy was missing. When we returned to church -- and Tyler's wailing finally stopped -- we were as relieved as he.

Another time, Lambie lingered in a cart at Sautter's grocery. Calling the store from home, I said we'd be right back to pick him up. When we arrived, there was Lambie, waiting for us in a brown grocery bag.

For our son, each reunion stirred untold joy: A smile broke through and tears dried; Earth returned to its axis.

I can't say precisely when the bond formed. Lambie arrived on Tyler's first Christmas; soon, everywhere that Tyler went, the lamb -- like Mary's -- was sure to go, even into bathtubs and sandboxes.

Sometimes, while fixing supper, I'd open a cupboard and see Lambie plopped inside a pan. Or I'd find him in a drawer or a shoebox. A constant highchair companion, he soon advanced to the table along with our son, sampling Tyler's food and earning a milky, wet mouth.

With such love, Lambie's white fluff became matted and dingy. His silk-lined ears frayed, an eye fell off, and his neck -- by which he was most often carried -- stretched to a string.

Lambie was in constant need of the washing machine's gentle cycle. During one such spin, half his stuffing came out; another time, his blue silk bow disappeared. And always, afterward, I had to sew the tip of his tail to secure its jingle bell.

When Tyler sensed the impending separation, he'd say, "No bath. Lambie all clean." But as soon as he saw I meant business, he'd stand on his little green chair and peek inside at the suds. His patience amazed me. He was right there, too, by the dryer when Lambie emerged.

No matter how trying his day, Ty could fall to sleep as long as one of Lambie's ears was in one hand and the thumb of his other hand was in his mouth.

I can't say when the bond loosened, or finally broke. One day, the earth must have appeared more firm under our son's foot, the sky closer to his head.

Our daughter, like Linus, once felt secure with her blanket, dragging it everywhere, holding a corner of it close to her mouth when she fell asleep. Grown up and gone, like her brother in Boston, she teaches at the University of Potsdam outside Berlin. Where do our children find security now? Where do any of us?

In parents, spouse, family and friends? In a job?

Every close friend and family member present at my mother's wedding, including her husband, is deceased. The school where she taught no longer exists.

Her youth has vanished. All former forms of security, gone, including her long-lost childhood toys that once kept her safe.

Yet, she endures. Perhaps, in the end, the only thing that can make us feel secure is the knowledge that nothing is secure, nothing is safe forever. Not even ourselves. Saintlike Mother Teresa -- who has enough heart for the whole world -- has a heart that is failing her. Aristotle Onassis -- who had enough wealth to buy an island, a fleet and a president's widow -- couldn't prevent his son's death or his own life from running out.

Nothing, except perhaps faith -- that assurance of things not seen -- can offer a sense of security.

When our son was young and his Aunt Martha was baby-sitting, they hunted two-and-a-half hours for Lambie without success.

Finally, at bedtime, Martha had Ty pretend that Lambie was right there beside him -- and he fell asleep.

Sometimes, all we need to feel secure is the memory of when we once felt safe.

Fiftieth Birthday

Midwinter I found myself face-to-face with a saguaro cactus.

"Note its tall, cylindrical stem," said the guide at Phoenix's Desert Botanical Garden. "A saguaro can grow fifty feet high and live two hundred years. It doesn't produce its first flower -- a large, white blossom -- until it's forty years old. It doesn't produce an arm until it's about seventy. A saguaro with several arms may be a hundred and fifty years old."

There in the Sonoran Desert my spirits rose. I looked with new interest -- and admiration -- at this symbol of mature productivity. I thought of a friend who encouraged her secretary to earn a college degree. "No way," the secretary protested. "By the time I finish I'll be at least forty."

"Look," my friend said. "You're going to turn forty anyway. Would you rather be forty with your degree or without it?"

The saguaro also reminded me of my mother, who grew

a painting arm and eye in her seventies. A few years ago, I discovered her drawings -- rigid renderings of her flower garden. I gave her art lessons for a birthday gift. Today she paints exquisite watercolors, devours art books, visits galleries. Even taking a walk with her is different. She notices things -- a gathering of light, a parade of shadows -- I would not have seen.

If my mother and the secretary and even the saguaro cactus had learned the art of evolving, maybe I could, too.

The desert is a fitting place to visit in the middle of life. In the past, leafy options filled my view. Now fewer, more singular outlines shape the future. Years can be sharp pruning shears. But they bring us to the core of things.

Writing this on the last day of my forty-ninth year, I was heartened by Anne Morrow Lindbergh's words in *Gift From the Sea:* ". . . the morning of life, the active years before forty or fifty, is outlived. But there is still the afternoon opening up . . . time at last for those intellectual, cultural and spiritual activities that were pushed aside in the heat of the race . . . a . . . second flowering, second growth."

The ability to adapt to shifting sands -- to change -- appears to be a secret of successful living. Goals help see us through.

"I think it's tremendously important for people to set goals," said the late Helen Hayes. "To drift along and just take what comes and pray that it'll get better all the time, that you will get better and better things, I think that's . . . like gambling your life, isn't it? It's like shooting the dice."

Like a schoolgirl, I stayed up late on the eve of my fiftieth birthday -- trying to write down goals, making a study of my life. I remembered the saguaro cactus. Under a sky of stars, did it dream of stretching up an arm?

I also thought of its faraway friend -- the gnarled apple tree outside my Columbus, Ohio, window. Branch after

184

branch has been cut away so only one arm now reaches skyward from its old, massive trunk.

"It's dead except for that one limb. You ought to cut the whole thing down," insists the nurseryman. But I can't. Come spring, a bird may build its nest in that one remaining branch. A few of its buds will flower. And in late summer a small offering of apples will fall to the ground. Reason enough for living.

Lipstick

"I have to tell you, because I'm the only one who will," my daughter announced.

"You already did," I reminded her. "You said my hair looks damaged."

"Yeah, it does," she said, "but this is about your lipstick."

"My lipstick?"

"You need a more contemporary look: less pink, more brown. Matte, not glossy."

"Change my lipstick?" I protested.

She asked too much. I'd stuck with a particular pink for more than twenty years. It was part of me. Other colors clashed with my skin tone, washed me out, even turned me green. The day I found "Palace Pink," I bought ten tubes on the spot. When it disappeared from the drugstore shelf a few years ago, I spent a few frantic weeks searching before we were reunited under a different brand name. I should have realized I was running against the tide. Pink was not "in" in the '90s; pink was passe.

Children, though not always gently, keep their parents young, keep them with-it. I used to notice how some older women applied lipstick above their lip line. When my mother committed that sin, I set her straight in a second. Perhaps I had become one of those "older women." Perhaps I had lost touch. Perhaps my pink lipstick made others, besides my daughter, cringe.

She led the way to a department store cosmetic counter. Like a cowering, wet puppy, I trailed behind her. Was I headed for another putdown? In the fall, when I was buying mascara, a saleswoman asked whether I'd ever tried a concealer.

"A concealer?"

"Yes," she said, handing me a gold tube. "It would help cover up all those lines under your eyes."

Suddenly, remembering that day, I hid my face with both hands and said to my daughter, "Maybe we should wait."

"Mom, don't pay attention to anything they might say," the twenty-five-year-old philosopher said. "It's all a sales pitch. They take away your self-confidence and then tell you you can buy it back for the price of their elixir.

"When I was only twenty," she said, "I went into a store for eyeliner. The clerk held up a mirror in front of my face and said, 'Look, so young and yet, already, so many wrinkles.' "

I dropped my hands as a saleswoman approached.

"I'm here to get my mom a more contemporary color of lipstick," said my daughter, still sounding parental.

The woman, dressed in a white lab coat, responded like an emergency medical worker: She flicked on a high-intensity light, aimed a magnifying mirror in my direction and began applying foundation to my face.

"But the lipstick," my daughter reminded her, trying to keep her focused.

The clerk examined my frosted, pink shade as I shifted from side to side. Finally she handed down the verdict:

"Actually," she said, "Mom is in. In fact, she's even a little ahead of her time: Pink is back, along with frost and shine."

I was speechless, my daughter dumbfounded. Like an old necktie, I'd been "out" so long, I was suddenly "in."

"But what about the brown look?" my daughter asked, doubting -- as did I -- that I could be on the cutting edge of anything.

"Brown-based tones and matte finish really took off five or six years ago," said the clerk. "Now the look is on its way out."

I smiled gleefully, straightening my shoulders and standing a little taller. My daughter shrank.

"It's all rather new -- pinks, peaches with shiny, frosted finishes," continued the woman, glancing at my mirrored reflection. "You're at the beginning of a trend."

If she'd stopped right there, she would have made my day. Instead she said, "The bimbo look is back."

Poetry Garage Sale

True to what I expect from my sister Karen, her garage sale is out of the ordinary.

She's "selling" her old poems.

First, to the trash, she says, she's "dragging all work lacking / central metaphors, all derivative / poems and ones which try to be / funny, but fail."

Down in the storeroom, she sorts through other poems overflowing their crates.

"This one is old-fashioned and rhymes, but someone might enjoy it," she says of an early effort. "I never did like that one's shape, and I've outgrown this view."

In the garage late at night, she groups and prices her bounty -- "starts of poems in an old clothes hamper / two for fifty cents / poems with expired shelf lives in a cracked crock / ten cents a piece."

The one about driving away from the farm that last time might be worth keeping, she thinks, as she slips it into her jeans.

With the same hope that "space will elicit new order," I follow her lead. Opening my desk drawer, overflowing with her poetry, I pull out a poem:

"Right here where I cook is where I'll write," Karen began nineteen years ago. "It is meet and right to prepare food for the soul / With no less care than salads and entrees. / Here where I grate and chop /. . . I'll apron my soul and set to work / Hewing my thoughts and honing my feelings / To a finer point than conversation. / Then when I serve them to you, garnished with verse, / Instead of fast food, short order conventions, / What you'll taste is me."

How could I throw out the forty-year-old version of her, the one who inspired me? I place it firmly in my "save" pile.

My sister, a passionate soul, skirted a midlife crisis by turning to poetry, the language of strong feeling. Though still a mother and wife, who played the violin and rode horses, she began to reflect on her experiences through writing. In the way that art fed her life, life fed her art.

"A poem begins with a lump in the throat, a homesickness or a love-sickness," Robert Frost observed. "It is a reaching-out toward expression; an effort to find fulfillment."

I think of Karen's poem that asks: "Who has not felt the heartbreak of a half step? / It catches my throat. / Music lies in the intervals, / not the lonely notes on either side. / How far the spaces are in pitch and time / creates the meaning, makes the mood. / So though you live in the country / while I must stay in town / doesn't matter half as much / as the song that sings between us."

I want to keep that poem, just as I do the one about her daughter: "You sleep so lightly beneath the quilt I sewed, / I can scarcely see your outline, / must pat my hand along the puff / as one gropes along the wall / in the night for the switch /. . . Lying straight and on your back, / you seem a mummy, a child

190

Pharaoh. / Your pale hair radiates across the pillow / like an ancient headress of the sun."

Better than any resume, her poems reveal the woman.

Why, for instance, does my sister's phone ring unanswered? "Gladly I live in the presence / of things left undone, / or how could I see / these fields, / yellow more and more, / or these hills, indigo blue? / I would miss storm clouds roiling like this tangle of mane beneath my hand, / the bright spurt of speed / as we race toward the elm. / Red baneberry would languish unseen; / I would never have considered / the possibilities of green."

Or this one, written after a daughter's graduation: "You're cast, kid, / you got the script, / you got technique, / you learned to improvise. / Somewhere along the way / you picked up special effects, / a sense of timing. You know what you think you want / and how to go for it. / I'm just the producer . . . so why do I sit here / at the back of the hall / calling 'Cut, cut!' / waving my hands wildly / in the dark?"

Hours later, I've not found one poem to throw out. Karen is harder on herself: Some lines that she plans to get rid of, she says, expose an appalling self-pity, mistake uniqueness for emotion or lack images. She softens when she comes across those fresh and straight from her heart. Yet, realizing they could only have been published at the time, she intends to discard them anyway.

I'd go to Wisconsin and "buy" her verses, every one -- for they hold the essence of my sister, our family. What if they were mistreated by strangers? I have to protect the poems, especially the one about my father's hands that used to look so young.

And the one about flower fields where "we braided daisy chains, / tied them to bridles, or wore them like crowns, / and glittering with gold dust, / cantered through / clover and yarrow and flowers so blue / only clouds told where fields left off, / and sky showed through."

The Midnight Kitchen

If my father had run for president, he could have said that he, like Abraham Lincoln, was born in a log cabin. His story of growing up in the new century, as a child of Norwegian immigrants, captivated me more than any fiction.

Something Dickensian wove through his losing both parents by age six, then being rescued just before he was sent to an orphanage; and his working his way through college and medical school.

Not simply his own stories, however, but those he told of his parents and the aunt and uncle who raised him stirred my soul. The tales gave me life, almost as much as he had, and filled my heart the way a family tree shapes heredity. After the storyteller died, I wished I'd listened harder, written down everything -- as the vivid became vague.

I had lost more than a father.

One recent evening I came across a tape whose faded, handwritten label I couldn't decipher. Busy, sorting and pitching, I put it aside. Hour after hour, I sensed an intrusion: "Play me."

Finally, close to midnight, I popped the cassette into a recorder. Suddenly, my father's voice, resonating across two decades, filled the kitchen.

Life, I realized, sometimes offers a second chance.

Stopped by death in 1992, Dad had been silenced by a stroke six years earlier. Yet, I could hear again his familiar voice, rich and clear, telling the old tales.

He was visiting me at the time, shortly after my sister had died. Wishing I had her on tape, and not wanting to make the same mistake, I placed a tape recorder in front of him.

"When my parents came to America in 1898," the seventy-one-year-old began, "opportunities in the Scandinavian countries were practically nil. Eventually, my father, who wanted to farm, brought his family to Wadena County in northwest Minnesota near Verndale, a little railroad crossing.

"Gudrun, my sister, could remember arriving at this deserted crossing in the dead of night," he continued. "My father had arranged for a covered wagon, with a cow tied to it, and a team of horses. Somehow, despite a thundering storm, they reached the farm ten to fifteen miles away."

The family moved into the log cabin, abandoned by previous homesteaders. In 1907, my father, the youngest of four children, was born. His father delivered him "because the weather was so bad that the woman who was supposed to couldn't get there."

My grandfather, struggling to add to his income, would go by covered wagon to the Red River Valley, the border between North Dakota and Minnesota, looking for extra work.

"One harvest when Dad was away," my father said, "fire leveled the new frame house that he had just built. . . .

Someone called out to 'save the baby,' which was me. Gudrun, who was about eleven, rolled me in a quilt. Reaching a knoll, she turned around to look at the house burning. Someone called, 'Where's Leif?' and she said, 'Right here in the quilt.' She looked, and there was no baby. She ran back, and there I was on the ground, only a few feet from the house. . . . Nothing was saved -- no clothes, nothing."

The family again found refuge in the old log cabin. Auntie Karen sent by freight from Eau Claire, Wisconsin, "a sugar barrel, which is a huge barrel much larger than a regular one, about the size of what they used to call a hogshead."

As my father's stories filled the midnight kitchen, I reached inside the barrel and helped his family unpack canned goods and spices, linens and blankets.

Standing by his younger self, I watched two men with leather straps lower his mother's coffin and, in less than a year, his father's into the earth.

Huddling outside a door, after the minister announced that the four children would go to an orphan asylum, I heard my great-aunt proclaim: "I'm not going to permit it. I'm taking them back to Eau Claire with me."

That night, not only did the old tales of my father live again -- but so did he; so did I; so did we.

Lifeline

My mother, my daughter and I form a line -- a lifeline. Here in my house, their visits -- like our lives -- overlap.

Mother arrives first. Greeting her at the back door, I'm stunned to see how faded her blue eyes have become, how they have paled since I was growing up -- or since she was growing up on a blooming prairie.

She and her friends would watch the setting sun smear the sky and dream of dresses the same color -- "sky-blue pink," they tried explaining to their mothers.

Sky-blue pink, an impossible shade.

Impossible like the blue into which I gaze. In their eighty-one years, her eyes have seen four babies take their first breath, and a grown daughter after she'd taken her last. They have discovered a husband dead after fifty-seven shared years of days and nights. They witnessed the Great Depression, World War II and other wars -- and, one by one, the loss of everyone from her childhood family.

The one on whom we all leaned now leans on us. The

one who remembered everything forgets as time plows rude paths.

Yet, the mother in her, concerned about me, wants to help, and the daughter in me, like a knee tapped for a reflex, responds. For a moment, we try on old roles and quickly smooth the wrinkles in our discarded costumes.

Then, wearing youth's seamless garment, my daughter arrives fresh from her first year of law school. She, whose hands we held when Mother and I took her for walks, is stronger than both of us. We marvel at her miraculous, still-new body moving freely through time.

Looking at the two of them, I see myself reflected, refracted: in Mother, what I will become; in my daughter, what I once was.

Was it so long ago that I, awaking from a nap, turned frantic, running from room to empty room, until I found my mother in the back yard? Beyond the fence lay a fairy-tale forest -- and the world -- fringed in gold.

Was it that long ago that I, running after my son or setting the table or going here, there and everywhere, carried my daughter on my hip?

A wall of twenty-eight years separates my mother from me; another twenty-eight-year wall divides me from my daughter. I sense diminishing energy on one side, a gathering force on the other -- as each of us holds onto her evolving place along the lifeline.

In the middle, with opposing pulls, I sometimes have trouble finding my footing. I almost lose my balance.

Mother leaves first. Each goodbye gives birth to: "Will we ever see each other again?"

Later that day, my daughter's boyfriend arrives. The next day, he sweeps her away.

"Are you going to give us a push like your parents would?" she asks as they head for the car.

I recall the ritual: Side by side, my parents placed their hands on the trunk, giving the car a little push down the drive. I leaned out the window, waving goodbye as they ran. This time, my daughter is the one waving.

"That's me," I say to myself, watching her go.

It is. And it isn't.

That evening, as I work in the garden, a robin and I are the only ones at home. Weeks ago she made a nest, now quivering with life, on top of the porch light. Relentlessly she feeds three gaping mouths.

Does she remember how one did such for her?

I return to my planting.

After a long while, I stand up -- realizing a unique sensation: I'm content in the moment, not longing for anyone or anything else. For an instant, letting go of the lifeline on either shore, I float, free.

I take in everything around me -- the sun gilding the hemlocks, the robin swooping back and forth, the sound of whirring tires slowing to a stop. Most of all, I see the sky -- not so much sky-blue pink, but a color all its own -- bending toward summer.

A Father's Wallet

Ten years ago on Father's Day, shortly after he woke up, my father suffered a stroke.

Painstakingly, he learned to walk again -- but not with the same strong stride. He relearned with his one good hand -- the one least used during his first seventy-nine years -- how to feed himself and dress himself, tie his Windsor knot and slip his wallet into his pocket.

Now and then, out of watery memory, words such as "Yes" or "Nice" or "Love you" would bubble to the surface.

Such feats gave me hope that these puzzle pieces eventually would form the man I knew.

Other signposts signaled a different person: His shuffle took on a tentative tilt; food increasingly fell from his fork. Even swallowing was no longer a simple reflex.

Yet a daughter's heart lagged behind her mind, refusing to learn the lesson.

Truth arrived in a restaurant.

After a family dinner, my father -- out of long habit --

reached for his brown leather wallet. The venerable patina, like the man himself, reflected years of good, honest work and gifts to others.

Yet, like its owner, the wallet looked a little worn with the passage of time. Gone were membership cards, credit cards and a driver's license. What remained were a few dollar bills, given Dad by Mother, to preserve his sense of autonomy.

Despite polite protests, he emptied the contents onto the table while she discreetly made up the difference. He smiled the smile of the perennial provider.

His arduous triumph counterbalanced my despair. In that moment, I sensed that all the love, money and medicine couldn't put my father together again.

Not the way he used to be, in the fullness of life, when each night he'd placed his wallet, watch and keys high on the bureau. Or, when each morning, gathering them up, he'd headed out the door.

Time and again, by opening his wallet, he opened the world -- movie tickets, rides at the country fair, trips on a ferry, ice-cream cones, new tires before a family vacation, gas for the car, room at an inn.

Reaching inside, he made the impossible possible -- our first television -- and bought us bushels of Jonathan apples, pumpkins and Christmas trees.

Once, as a child, I pulled a chair over to his bureau and climbed up to see what I could see. Though I put his pipe to my mouth and pretended to be him, I couldn't bring myself to open his wallet. Would I be stealing if I stole just a glance?

At that height, the air thinned.

With a beating heart I clambered back down.

As far as I know, the only one of his four children ever to examine his wallet was my brother -- after our father's death. My brother mentioned the wallet during an October visit.

"Did I ever show you this?" he asked, handing me a slip of paper that looked as if it had been clipped from a magazine decades before.

"I found it in Dad's wallet. He must have carried it forever."

Again the wallet opened up a world -- this time, my father's -- as I read the words on how to live a good life, with oneself and with one's fellow man, so that one could go in peace.

What was on his mind the day he cut it out? How often did he refer to it?

He tried to lead such a life. And he went in peace, I thought, as the image of hands, folded in death, came back to me. How much, I wondered, had to do with a clipping in his wallet?

Over Memorial Day weekend my son flew home for a visit. Working as a summer clerk in a law firm, he emerged from the flight wearing professional clothes -- a new suit and tie, and even wing-tips.

I continued to admire this and that, taken aback by his adult demeanor.

When he proudly pulled out a new leather wallet, unetched by time, and searched my face for a response, I couldn't speak. I found no words.

Last Day of School

Like a treasure washed up on time's shore, the small, gold cardboard box sits on my desk. Tiny seashells decorating the lid surround a photograph -- no bigger than a thumbnail -- of my son at age five. He cut out the circular image from his class picture and decorated the top. How well I remember that long-ago face, with the swirl of cowlick above the forehead, and the blue-and-white Western shirt he wore on the first day of kindergarten in 1973.

Just before my firstborn rode off on his bike, he let his dad shoot the commemorative photo. I didn't give a thought to his final destination -- lying endlessly ahead.

Forever arrived with a phone call.

"Mom," he said, "I wanted to call you on my last day of school. It all came to an end today."

His journey that began so long ago at Highland Elementary in Sylvania, Ohio, reached its conclusion -- after a four-year stint in public service -- at a Boston law school.

His sister had shown up at his apartment that day to take his picture. She had with her a brown-bag lunch filled with his old-time favorites -- a peanut-butter-and-jelly sandwich, Fritos and bubble gum. The note inside read: "Happy last day of school ever."

At the end of his last class, as he filled out a course evaluation form, she quietly sneaked in and snapped another picture. Good for her, I thought. Everyone celebrates the first day of school and graduation. Yet, who honors the day when one reaches the finish line?

Something ended for me, too. As I talked on the telephone -- at the same desk where I used to fill out school forms and sign permission slips -- I picked up the little box.

My son was almost a year old when I carried him with me to the Spring Fling at the neighborhood school. "Four years -- an eternity -- before he starts kindergarten," I remember thinking gratefully.

For any parent, that first day arrives all too soon -- as does the end of the ride.

We often announce to family and friends, "We're having a baby."

No one says, "We're having a kindergartner (or a teenager or an adult)."

Yet, we are.

"I remember in third grade when I realized there was only one month to go before summer vacation," my son said. "Then I thought, 'I'm going to have to go back next year and the next and on and on . . . I'll have to go to school until I'm practically my parents' age.' It seemed like forever, like it would be my whole life."

Even he was surprised to have come full circle.

Studying his photograph, surrounded by white shells, I recalled an ancient medicine wheel, with its circle of white stones.

American Indians compare life to a wheel -- birth and death, beginnings and endings. Always spinning around the wheel, we continually arrive at a place of birth, of beginnings. We reach times, too, when we stop and center ourselves.

I saw such a wheel in Arizona, where a guide referred to middle age as the "path of power where we earn a living and honor the responsibilities of a material world, where we care for the young and the old. Children and grandparents travel paths more spiritual -- which is why there is the closeness between them."

Years ago, my children were dependent on me. One day I may become dependent on them. At some point, our paths will intersect. Have they now?

Phone Call to a Son

All day, I was afraid to call my son at his new job. I had thought nothing of phoning him or leaving a message on his answering machine when he attended college. During his younger years, I'd call him in from play or down for dinner. Yet, I was afraid to pick up the phone and call the child whose newborn self I'd once cupped in my hands.

Even more, I feared that something had happened to him -- nonsense, my rational self insisted.

My emotional side concluded otherwise: His sister, who used to live nearby in Boston, had moved to New Orleans. His girlfriend had taken a job in Los Angeles. If some misfortune had occurred, how would anyone know?

He usually doesn't let a week go by without some communication. In the two weeks that had passed, I'd already left a couple of "Hope all is well" messages at his apartment.

What's a mother to do?

As you step over Legos and Beanie Babies, you might be dreaming of the day when your motherly worries will end.

I don't know how to tell you: That day may not come.

For now, at least, when you put your children to bed, you know where they are -- under the same roof, safe and sound.

Nothing, not even lectures about giving children roots and wings, can prepare a parent for such a strange passage.

He definitely grew wings.

Mine, clipped long ago, left me fretting at the empty nest.

At this stage -- many years after car pools and sleepovers -- I had envisioned myself free as a bird, out on the town, not lurking about the house, waiting for a call from a suddenly ancient child.

All day, whenever I entered the kitchen, I stared at the phone: "Call him at work; hear his voice; be reassured," it tempted. A few times I started to dial, then hesitated.

A curtain had closed, echoing louder than the snipping of apron strings.

Whereas once, in midnight hours of panic, Dr. Spock might have rescued me, I treaded alone.

"Who's calling, please?" asked the receptionist at the law firm.

"Oh," I said as my son's life flashed before my eyes.

Suddenly I saw my old lunch partner enjoying a peanut-butter-and-jelly sandwich. Many of his classmates, he said that noon, wanted to be president. He thought maybe he did, too.

"When I go to the White House to see you," I said, "the guard will stop me at the gate and phone the Oval Office.

" 'Mr. President,' he'll say, 'there's a lady here who claims to be your mother. She says she has your peanut-butter-and-jelly sandwich.'

" 'That's her,' you'll say. 'Send her up.' "

And we both laughed.

Finally, I answered the question: "This is his -- mother," I said, cringing at the last word. Had I unwittingly dashed any impression he was trying to make?

The gates swung open as I heard a familiar voice say, "Hi, Mom."

"I know you're busy and can't talk," I said.

"Actually, I am in the middle of something, but can I call you back?"

At ten-thirty that night, still at work, he did. I could barely concentrate on all his news, knowing he had yet to leave for supper.

The mother in me who had needed to call now wanted to hang up and let him get on with his life.

Later, drifting off to sleep, content, I recalled the cooing of homing pigeons raised by a childhood neighbor. I remembered how I used to pester him with questions, watch him tag the carrier birds, wait for their return. Once, when one pigeon was long overdue and we had just about given up hope, he spotted a speck in the sky.

Beside myself with joy, I watched it draw closer and closer, looming larger and larger, coming home.

Pansy Patch

Who knows how the longing starts?

Like a plant making its way to the surface, a notice in the Toledo newspaper sent forth a shoot: "William Freitag, director of student and community services, is retiring after thirty-four years."

In 1977 he was "Mr. Fweitag," a speech therapist who taught my first-grade daughter and other children how to pronounce their "r's."

Or maybe I started remembering because of an old folder I found, the one holding the 1971 roster of a Lamaze childbirth education class. Inside were listed the names, addresses and phone numbers of seven couples, including the due dates of their expected babies.

Next to "8-6-71," the instructor had jotted down my daughter's birth date of five days earlier.

Attached were my handwritten reminders on what to pack for the hospital: loose change for phone calls, stamps for birth announcements and, of course, baby clothes.

Then again, perhaps the feeling unfolded with a note:

"Dear Mom," she wrote as her graduation from law school approached, "When I saw this card, I thought of you and me planting pansies. I liked pushing 'em out of their flats.... You'd ask me, 'What color now?' and I'd say, 'A yellow one' or 'A blue one.' You'd ask, 'Where do we want this one?' and I'd pick a spot -- until all the flats were spent. Happy spring."

Who knows when we bought that first flat, or where? Or how one simple afternoon grew into a spring ritual? What's important is that when I called her from play, she and her friends came running. After clearing away winter's wreckage, we turned the soil.

A pansy patch taught responsibility: If the plants weren't watered, they'd wilt and die; if not pinched back, they'd grow long and leggy. Flowers, standing for "thoughtfulness," offered a lesson in sharing: They could be picked and given as gifts by the tiniest hand.

Each year, though, saw her less close to the ground, less eager to help, as the universe beyond the yard beckoned.

Other graduations -- from grade school, high school and college -- have been as different as the changing child.

Where did she go? The one who once wrote, after I directed a student production of *Tom Sawyer*, "Dear Mom, I thout your plae tom soyr was grate"? Or who, some years later, left a note on the kitchen counter: "Out riding bike or at Lesli's"? Or who, when she saw me act fearful, helped me become stronger by encouraging me to be strong for her?

Why, as I pack for her latest graduation, am I reminded of once filling a suitcase with her newborn clothes?

"Hello, you don't know me," I said to Pat Shaw on the telephone, "but twenty-seven years ago this summer we were in the same Lamaze class. You're the only one that I've been able to reach, since your phone number is still the

208

same."

While she talked, I remembered warm Monday evenings in a church basement, the windows flung open to find a breeze -- six weekly sessions where we learned to "avoid the perception of pain."

"I see by the instructor's notation -- 7-30-71 -- that you were the only one in the class who delivered on your due date."

Boy or girl? I inquired.

"A son, Tom," she said, offering to let me talk to him.

"That's all right," I said, fumbling for words, wondering why I suddenly needed to go back to my daughter's beginning -- and his.

After we hung up, I realized I was unsure what to pack for the rest of the trip -- for a life, more and more, without her.

No weekly course exists for that, no list of what to carry, no sure way to "avoid the perception of pain."

Just try to keep busy, I tell myself, and look forward to the times we'll meet along the way.

Meanwhile, there are pansies to plant.

The Window Shade

Remember how, like the morning sky, time once towered endlessly before us?

Remember, too, when we saw just a nick of window shade trim the top of the window, blocking out a sliver of blue? Year by year, the blue disappears behind the descending shade.

Eventually, we tell ourselves, we'll see more shade than sky. Then what?

One day, my friend JoAnn sensed her room growing darker. She decided to visit those who had shaped her life -- to express her love and to give or ask forgiveness.

"I don't want to wait until either they or I have cancer, with only a few months to live," she said. "I want to go now, in the midst of life, to say goodbye. Then, no matter what happens, I will have said what I had to say."

Some of those close to her had already vanished. So that summer she journeyed to see her parents, sisters, childhood friends and college roommates.

210

Will this be the summer of our goodbyes -- to take stock, to put life in perspective, to talk openly with family and friends?

Pilgrimage, rather than vacation, might be a better word for such a journey -- not so much the chance to "get away from it all" as the chance to "get closer to it all" and find new insights.

In the half-light of the middle of my life, two people already are gone -- my sister Sonja, who died in 1977, and my father, who died in 1992.

I wish I could travel the landscape back to them. I wish I could tell my sister that what she told me -- "Just do it" -- about achieving a goal has become a Nike ad. She was ahead of her time. I smile when I recall the words she said during our last conversation.

And I wish I could tell her I'm sorry -- sorry for the times when, as kids, we'd be talking or watching television or quarreling and she'd scrunch up her face in a grimace.

"What's wrong?" I'd ask.

"Just a shooting pain in my leg," she'd say.

Though I didn't dispute her comment, I used to think she was overreacting, dramatizing, pretending that her leg hurt to get attention. Now that I know more about diabetes and the havoc it plays with one's circulatory system, I'm amazed that she didn't complain more about pain, didn't rail more against her illness.

I wish I could tell my father that not until I became a parent did I realize something he'd done for me. Although I was daughter number three, born three days after his birthday, I never thought that my sex and timing might have been off-target. Never in my life, not even in a joking way, did he make me feel unwanted, make me think that he might have preferred a boy.

Instead, I was king -- or, rather, queen -- of the hill, as he carried me about like his mascot. I can still feel, against my cheek, the voice resonating deep in his chest, the starched shirt collar at his tanned neck. I last saw his hands folded in death, but I remember them young and active, teaching me how to ride my bike or grabbing the handles of his doctor's bag.

In the morning of my life, with a flick of his wrist, he'd lift the window shades -- telling my sisters and me, and later my brother, to rise and shine: "It's a beautiful day in Kenosha today."

Other times, as he lathered up, becoming a bearded Santa in front of a mirror, my mother would let in the light -- pausing to rub our shoulders, smoothing back a lock of our hair -- before she went downstairs to fix breakfast.

Today, the children who rose long ago in those bedrooms are gone. My mother alone remains in the house. During the summer I will travel to Wisconsin to stay a while and say what I have to say: I will never forget her courage, for instance, when my father, far away, was recovering from tuberculosis.

Because she was strong, we felt safe. Because she believed he'd get better, we believed. And he did.

Sometimes, raising the window shade today, I remember how my parents once showed us the whole world shimmering beyond the sill.

Memorial Day

The long, lone whistle of a train always takes me back along the track to Seventh Avenue and its graveyard.

In my dreams, prairie grasses part and sand dunes stir, as the engine stops to let me climb aboard. I take a window seat, and the train pulls forward under a flag of stars.

"Tickets," calls the conductor moving from car to car. I hand him mine. Destination: home. Date: Memorial Day.

Pressing my forehead against cool glass, I see a farmhouse's lonely light fight the darkness. Once, weeping torches lit this midnight way as Abraham Lincoln's funeral train shouldered him home to the prairie. From Chicago the Alton Railroad cradled his flag-draped coffin on the final run to Springfield.

We move on to Wisconsin -- skimming past pine in shadowy light. If I were blindfolded, the station's air alone -- a mingling of May and Lake Michigan -- would tell me I was home.

Floating across town, I glimpse the grade school where a

213

flag once waved forty-eight stars, where we once waved at General Douglas MacArthur.

In Library Park I see the statue of Lincoln, who's seated and reading a book. My father used to lift me up there to sit in his lap. Later I climbed there myself and pretended Lincoln told a story just to me. How important I felt, sitting next to a president.

Back then I didn't know Memorial (or Decoration) Day had first been observed three years after his burial in 1865, when flowers were placed on the graves of Union and Confederate soldiers. I only knew that on May 30 I couldn't sit on Lincoln's lap, because the statue was dressed up with a wreath.

Dawn lifts as I pass the old house on Seventh. Soon the flag will fly above the front door. Growing up, my sisters and I picked wildflowers to decorate the tombstones in an overgrown woods -- the abandoned cemetery -- behind our house. The century-old stones of the town's early settlers were so worn that we had to rub the ancient inscriptions with dirt to better read the names and dates and beloved-by-whoms.

Life's forgotten foot soldiers, they had no one left to remember them. Except us. We, self-appointed caretakers, fashioned bouquets, straightened fallen stones, cleared weeds and thorny brush. More than once we held our own spontaneous services. We included these people in our make-believe, wondering who they were and what kind of lives they had led.

I felt sorry for the souls we had to leave behind. But each May 30 our family filed into the neat and trim Green Ridge Cemetery down the street from our scraggly one in the woods. Flags flapped against white markers and the bright, mowed grass. A band played hymns, and the bugle sounded taps.

Most of the time, life follows a daily track, rocking us along in familiar fashion -- calendars to keep, errands to run. Ceremony brings rolling steel to a stop. In the steaming sigh that follows, we pay rapt attention instead of rushing by.

Before leaving my old hometown, I drift back to the house on Seventh, where railroad tracks ran behind the abandoned cemetery, where each night I would fall asleep to the sound of a train's whistle. Back then, it always carried my thoughts to the future.

The telephone rings me out of my dream. It's Mother calling to say that yesterday she planted geraniums by my sister's grave. "And when I got home from Green Ridge," she says, "Monfils Monuments called to say your dad's stone is in and ready to set."

Unlike in childhood, I wish I didn't know the inscription.

Sixtieth Wedding Anniversary

"What would you like to send?" the florist asked.

"White peonies," I replied.

On my parents' wedding day, peonies -- free for the gathering from against a backyard fence -- were all that a family pulling out of the Depression could afford.

"And how would you like the card to read?"

I couldn't say, "Happy sixtieth wedding anniversary" -- as my father, who died two years ago, wasn't there to share it.

"Just write, 'Thinking of you,' " I said.

After the flowers were sent, I realized what I should have said: "Thinking of you both."

Destiny drew them together: He was traveling the unpaved roads in an old Chevrolet; she was riding a bus out of her way to fulfill a favor. My mother first saw my dad when he "burst through the door" of her brother's apartment in Portage, Wisconsin.

"He's framed in the doorway of my mind for all time --
like a painting," she said. "He had come from visiting
Auntie Karen in Eau Claire. When he reached a crossroad,
he flipped a coin to see if he should accept the invitation for
a weekend with my brother and his wife -- or return home
to Kenosha."

Mother -- tempted by a dance at the student union on the
eve of her senior year in college -- also had felt torn about
accepting the invitation. Yet, her brother and sister-in-law
needed a fourth for bridge. At least that's what they said.
Reluctantly, she traveled from Madison to Portage.

When she first saw my dad after his long car trip -- "rum-
pled, dusty, hair uncombed" -- she found him instantly
appealing.

She later learned that he had felt the same.

"There was immediate attraction," she recalled. "We were
transported."

Feelings blossomed into love; love grew into a fifty-
seven-year union.

During their fifty-first year of marriage, my father suffered a stroke. He could no longer speak, but Mother "could
read his face and outstretched arms."

"My memory . . . is of him framed in the kitchen doorway
as he paused there each morning, waiting for our hug and
a kiss. He would always be smiling, dimples and all."

I called her on their anniversary. The peonies had
pleased her, prompting her to relive more family lore -- such
as their first dinner date.

My dad, then a young doctor, "launched into a descrip-
tion," she said, "of an operation for a retrocecal appendix,
using spoons and forks -- knives, even -- drawing pictures
on a prescription pad, explaining all in detail. I learned that
lesson so well," she recalled, "that every time it took longer

for an appendectomy I would say, 'It was retrocecal, wasn't it?' We would both smile and remember our first dinner date."

During two previous phone conversations, Mother had mentioned a rose bush -- the oldest in her garden.

"You know the one -- the pink one we brought with us forty-five years ago when we moved," she said, as if for the first time. "It's the loveliest it's ever been. You wouldn't believe how many roses it has. I can count them from here looking out the window: One, two . . ." -- climbing again to number fifteen.

"And there must be more on the side I can't see, so that makes at least twenty."

Why was the story so much on her mind?

I was about to interrupt when suddenly she offered a new tendril.

"Your father brought it along from the old house because I was so sad."

"What?" I asked, riveted by the twist.

"After the moving van left," she said, "and we were pulling out of the driveway, I burst into tears."

" 'What's wrong?' he asked, stopping the car.

" 'I don't want to leave my rose bush. It's my only one, and it's in bloom.'

" 'Well, then, we won't.'

"With that," she recalled, "he hopped out of the car, dug up the bush -- and planted it in our new garden."

Forty-five years later, better than my store-bought peonies, my father's gift remains rooted in love.

I sensed his presence -- like the roses on the other side of the bush.

My parents are still together. They're just on other sides of the same door.

His Mother's Keeper

Mother was thirty-six when she and my father moved their young daughters and infant son into the new house. Today, the cherry tree Dad planted almost fifty years ago reaches the upstairs porch. His martin house has vanished, leaving a white pole to pierce the sky.

A Jet Ski sits in the garage. Bach and Tanya Tucker take turns on a compact disc player in the living room, where on Sundays, the television is tuned in to Nascar Events. My parents always said that Chris -- their only son -- would keep them young.

Two years ago, after working in California for two decades, my brother, now forty-seven, returned home to Wisconsin. His visit has turned into a long-term stay. While looking for a job, he found one -- caring for our mother.

"I now realize," he told me at the time, "that Mom put up a good front on the phone, appearing to be in better shape than she actually was."

He was alarmed, along with my sister and me, at the sudden onset of her short term memory loss.

"I forget so much," she told me on one of my visits, "I don't have the recall that I used to . . . Chris remembers everything, reminds me about everything."

Regretting that he couldn't spend more time at home during Dad's final years, Chris vowed to help. My big, burly brother, who once played football and used to ride a motorcycle, has become a caregiver.

"He's been like a saint who's come into my life," our eighty-two-year-old mother said more recently. "He does all the shopping, the cooking, the laundry (he brings it up and I put it away) . . . I haven't had to drive since he's been here. . . . He shovels the snow, mows the grass.

"I don't know why I should have turned into somebody who doesn't do anything anymore," said Mom, who always worked harder than anyone I knew. "Yet, as long as he does it, I accept it and am glad."

To run errands or pay the bills or answer her social correspondence, the two have a ritual.

"Each morning," Mom told me, "Chris calls up the stairs, 'Is there anybody up there who'd be interested in a little breakfast?'

"I come down in my bathrobe and he's got it all set out -- strawberries, bananas, cereal, orange juice, coffee and my pills."

Last summer, Chris helped her recover from a broken leg. After he took her home from the hospital, her leg in a cast, he took apart her bed and set it up in the den. Within hours, he'd made the house accessible to a wheelchair.

Each meal tray bore a bouquet from her garden, each day brought his encouragement. Over time, he urged her to resist staying in bed and use her wheelchair; after she was fitted with a walking cast, to resist the wheelchair and use a walker; and, finally, to resist her walker and walk freely.

She is fully recovered.

He drives her to doctor and hair appointments, takes her out to eat, even accompanies her to the opera. He's taught her how to speed dial on an updated telephone, how to use a cordless model as a pager. In her closet and bedroom, he's installed light bulbs that turn off automatically.

His letters fill me in: "Today I watered your plant. . . . It looks real nice in the house. . . . Mom goes next door to Nancy's on Saturday for a bridal shower. Mom continues to improve day by day -- sort of. She still has her moments."

While Chris worries about her -- why she no longer likes to paint or read or play the piano -- she worries about him.

"Believe me, he has not had it easy," Mom frets. "I think at times it must be very sad for him."

My sister and I worry, too. We urge our brother, who has dropped out of the workaday world, to look for a paying job and have caregivers visit the house -- or use an adult day care center -- to assist. Would we be as concerned if he were a daughter and not a son?

In March, after she waited for a friend who never appeared, he wrote: "Another case of Mom getting signals crossed. Seems to be the norm these days. Bringing in outside help would just present more opportunities for even more crossed signals. So would day care, I believe."

He found solace in reading John Daniel's *Looking After, A Son's Memoir*.

"An excellent book," Chris wrote. "It's about a son taking care of his mother who is afflicted with memory loss in her waning years."

In June, Chris confirmed our worst suspicions: "The doctors now say that she definitely has Alzheimer's."

No wonder every time he takes her for a ride on her favorite road that "hugs the lake," she asks again, "What kind of tree is that?"

No wonder he has to tell her, as if for the first time, "It's a willow."

Although she might share the same story three times in a brief exchange, the three of us take heart knowing that our mother doesn't yet fit the layman's prime example of Alzheimer's: not one who forgets where she left the key but one who forgets the key's purpose.

We also take heart that a new drug might slow the most insidious, final phase of the disease.

Recently, my brother bought two new lamps for the empty bedroom across the hall from his.

"Even though no one's in there," he told me, "I leave them on a lot. They make the room seem alive."

That's what Chris does for the house where two, instead of six, now reside. He brings it to life.

And, at forty-seven, he continues to keep my mother young -- buying her a corsage and taking her to alumnae day at the girls school where she taught for fifteen years or, when her leg was broken, pushing her in the wheelchair on the power of his in-line skates.

In the spring, asleep in my old room, I awoke to the sound of the cherry branches brushing against the house.

Though I didn't hear a clock ticking, I sensed the great sweep of time -- from the day my mother moved us into the new house until that windy night.

The walker outside her bedroom door stood sentinel where Chris had placed it "just in case." I spotted it before dawn as I tiptoed downstairs.

Proud? I cannot tell you how proud I am of my brother, and how proud and grateful Dad would be.

In the still house, I wrote a note to Mom and Chris, left it on the kitchen table and headed home.

Your Finest Hour

You're out there -- wondering what it all means, how it all adds up.

You're thinking that nobody cares.

You crave sleep, having been awake most of the night with a newborn, yet you're sorting laundry. With the kids at school and the baby taking a nap, you're pulling lint off the clothes.

Suddenly, life seems to have been reduced to the white specks that cling to socks.

Or you're waiting for a repair crew to fix the refrigerator.

The company couldn't say when it would have someone there -- other than "morning" or "afternoon."

Some days, you handle it; other times you want to scream into the telephone.

Don't businesses realize that you have commitments, too? Having to put your life on hold, from eight a.m. to noon or from noon to five p.m., makes you feel trapped -- ordinary.

Maybe you've read Lucille Clifton's *An Ordinary Woman*, in which she speaks of being "plain as bread / round as a cake." She expected to be "smaller than this, / more beautiful, / wise in Afrikan ways, / more confident."

Perhaps when you read, "i had expected more than this / i had not expected to be / an ordinary woman," you said, "Yes, I feel exactly the same."

Someday, looking back to this time of managing car pools and taking out a loan to pay for your daughter's flute and packing lunches and making everyone else's day work, while your dreams -- when you can remember them -- fade, you'll realize what you really were, who you really are.

You are the hub, the wheel.

Life flows from you: You nurture it and send it out each day, and it returns gladly to you.

You attend athletic events and give birthday parties and make all the holidays happen.

Even now, you're thinking you won't be ready for Thanksgiving, let alone Christmas; you can't.

You will, though.

Anybody, you tell yourself, could do what you are doing.

So you dream -- of becoming a missionary or joining the Peace Corps. You want to feel needed, as if your life is making a difference.

You work at home -- and maybe part time or full time outside.

You marvel at how roles begin to shift: children becoming parentlike, parents becoming like children asking for advice.

A daughter gives you a briefcase to spur you on; a son spray-paints a message on the wall of a window well: "to the world's best mom -- I love you."

Just as time turns and they head out the door, you'll realize that you were given the best that life can give.

For now, though, you remain in the trenches, worrying that you don't have enough to go around.

You give more than you realize -- and you are learning as you go, disappointing yourself one day, starting over the next.

All the while, you seem to stay the same, while your children grow and change, their bodies and minds reinventing themselves even in sleep.

You will not have time to reflect as they go through the revolving years of childhood and exit. Still, someday, in the growing quiet, you will think about all those dinners through the decades, the gathering and sorting of clothing and attitudes, the misunderstandings and understandings.

One day, a letter carrier or the telephone will bring word of thanks or an insight.

A daughter, perhaps sewing the straps on her ballet shoes, will say that she feels like you (who used to sew for her, autumn after autumn).

Suddenly, as she feels like you, you will feel like your mother. You will lose yourself, merging into the larger scheme of the generations.

In that moment, you will find yourself. You will realize that the anonymous, fragmented work on the front of daily life has made you not ordinary but extraordinary.

I want you to know that now. Celebrate yourself.

Trust me: Someday you will look back and understand that this is, this was, your finest hour.